Drive Me Insane

Maddie. C

Paperback ISBN: 979-8-89778-071-6
Ebook ISBN: 979-8-89965-911-9

The K and W's of DMI

Author note : This novel is short and spicy and is intended for readers above the ages of 18+ Everything is with consent and meant for fun.

The following story contains different topics from the category BDSM and more. This is in no way shape or form meant to teach or anything else beyond—Reading for Fun!

Reader's discretion is advised, you have been warned.

DEDICATION

*To those who love being on their knees and being called,
'A good girl.' They are waiting for you.*

Chapter 1

One weekend away in one of the hottest places I knew. Stuck with a bunch of assholes I rather not have met again, especially after last time.

Ok, maybe they weren't *all* asses. Some were decent and were sort of making it up to me. Key word being sort of since they were more or less trying to get on my brother's nerves by coming near me with so called dirty intentions, as Chase put it. Speaking of brothers! I glanced at Chase who is laughing at something one of his friends said before throwing a beach ball around at one of the other guys. Luca had gracefully caught right as he fell under the water.

He was wearing a bright pair of red shorts and his hair was the main event, easy to spot as he pretend to drawn. Dark red hair with black ends that reminded me of a fox. Several piercings around his face, one in his nose, two snake bites underneath his lower lip. His left ear is covered in piercings, too. An industrial, a helix. I assumed it is called that since my best friend had one and she never stopped talking about it. There are also several other ones along the side of his ear going from the lobe up. A spider web tattoo peaked from the inside of his ear shell with a huge spider on his neck.

Then there is Cole. He is the level-headed one of the team. Calm and collected with no way of getting near him unless it is he who was gathering information from you. Cole stayed quiet in the corner of the pool, reading a book under a wide umbrella keeping his light skin safe from the frying sunlight and occasionally, I would catch him staring at the others as they were laughing in the pool. More precise, my brother. I knew Cole was gay, we all do. I just didn't expect for someone to crush on my brother.

As his sister, I know Chase way better than others do. Chase Brentwood is chaos in human flesh. An utter ball of fire just like our father used to be. He can be easily cracked under the right pressure, easily controlled. Mom was calm and collected and would always be able to bring dad back down from his chaotic episodes.

Jax is swimming fast behind Luca, he slaps the beach ball back over to my brother and then pushes Luca down in the water again. His wet dark blond hair covering his icy gray eyes. Several small tattoos cover his back and chest. Like a teddy bear he got for someone. The tattoo was a symbol to remember this certain somebody by with an A in the middle of the teddy's belly. A half moon on his shoulder, a skull and other odd designs. His back had this writing in old Latin going down his spine, a snake covered his left lower back side and the tail wrapped around—or more like coiled through the words. And then there was a cross at the top of his nape. The kind that the devil in human skin talking on the phone behind me also has.

Chase said that they all had gotten one in different places and the meaning behind it is that it's a symbol of protection as well as to check if it was one of their own if ever something happened.

I spotted someone walking inside the house and heading straight for Santino who placed his phone down and looked up at the man dressed in black. Bodyguards. Something was in his hand, something small and round before Santino took it, looked at it and handed it back with a rough push.

It was odd how there were so many guards around, lurking about. Yet in reality, you barely see them unless they came in and reported whatever they had to, to Santino. Even back in New Richdale where Chase and I live. Guards surround the modern vila my brother bought and installed high tech security to ensure I am always safe whenever he isn't around. Sweet and fucking annoying since trying to go to parties ended up being a lot harder with so much *safety* around.

"Calm your shit down, or I will calm you down myself." I looked back again. The voice of someone I thought I'd never see again gleamed like a distant vision as he spoke to whoever was on the other end of the line. It is a sin to be that fucking gorgeous. It just has to be. Santino Da Costa was and is a fucking demon straight from hell. Lucifer's perfect spawn. And the reason why we were here in the first place was because of his birthday. And the reason why I am here? I lost a bet with my brother about me coming here. He said that if I managed to find some sort of activity for the weekend that could keep me out of the house instead of my studio painting all day or sneaking to a party with my friends, then he would leave me be.

Sadly for me, when your brother springs the sudden news two days before the weekend and at midnight, too. It leaves you with one day of trying to find something to do. No spots were left open for the camping activities during the summer that I could have joined if I had known on time. Not to mention, there was no place for any art classes I could join as a teacher, either.

Chase said it's so I could see everyone again. Saying that last time we met—and the only time—had been a fluke since their mission had gone bad, very fast. It was the first time they had an official set team with a team leader instead of their actual boss giving orders. And Jax having come from a war spot where he has only seen death, made it harder tho trust everyone since he had met several men who had played the roles of moles in his old team.

My brother is part of a special ops group that deals with many different issues to sum it up. They knew how to hack, they knew the weapon handling, the big shot killers you never hear about, they were the ones who go after them. Though when that happens, there is a whole team of men not just these five crazies. This is the first time all of them are free with no missions to bother them in two, three years. A moment where they could all come together instead of talking on the phone or be sent in smaller teams out. It also fitted perfectly since it fell on Santino's twenty-seventh birthday as well. I couldn't help glare at the horse of a man as I merger my failed attempt at trying to not be here. Santino is tall, with tattoos covering his entire body all the way up his neck. Dark eyes with specks of gold. Black hair shaved short all around.

He looks like something straight out of a dark book where he was the villain. Muscles flexing as he spoke on the phone, his fist tightening and then relaxing. A large ring shined on his thumb that had a crest of sorts engraved into the cold material. I had seen a few of them up close during the time I worked at the art gallery. Each of those rings had a family story, they were heirlooms. A key to the upper world not just anyone could be part of. I was curious how Santino had one.

Why did he have one? Santino is an orphan, raised by a sister alongside a few other kids down in Portugal from what Chase told me. There is so little I know of him that every new detail manages to catch my attention. San used to operate the largest base in New Richdale and occasionally he would be come down to Spain to take care of the base here before it became his permanent spot. Our first meeting was a shitty one, one that left me hating him so much so that I didn't even wish him a happy birthday nor did I get him a present when we met this morning.

I sighed. Back then, Chase had requested my help. Since I befriended lots of rich people during my student job at the art house of New Richdale, I knew lots of people. I knew where most of the rich fools hung out, who they were friends with, and their favorite ways to skip time. So it was no surprise when I got invited to hang out with some of those rich people who may look innocent but had other plans for me. At first, San seemed ok with me, tolerating my presence at the time when he came down to my house.

Besides the very evident glare towards the world, he seemed to be ok with my company. The second Santino had seen me walking out of Chase's car though, dressed in a little black dress with a lace corset top, he had lost it. I had not given them any time to think about it as I grabbed a small earpiece and left through the crowd, going inside and started looking for this person they needed information on. In the end, they got what they needed, only to have things go down a moment later.

Guns erupted into a dance of hellfire around me and bodies hit the floor one after the other.

Gang members had joined the party and no one had any idea about it. Which pissed Santino off because he was meant to know these things. At first, I wanted to believe it was because I ended up hurt badly, with broken fingers and deep cuts.

Looking back at the demon after a moment of glaring at my brother. I find his eyes locked on me. And for some reason, things felt different now. More tense, more chaotic, darker and something about him was screaming louder than it did back then. Santino is dangerous, he is someone who has blood on his hands and I knew that, Chase warned me about it even. Told me to stay out of his way and here he was, dragging me down to Spain to spend the weekend with him and his friends.

Why? I had no damn clue.

"Nova! Come jump in the water." I looked away from Santino to look back at the others. Shaking my head, I stood up and walked inside the house, past the devil. I know he is watching, I also know how much I changed. I no longer was that young naive girl who tried being kind. I outgrew that phase long ago now. The black bikini I wore with heart-shaped rings between my full breasts pulling them together is a contrast to the oversized shirts and hoodies that kept my figure hidden years ago. I no longer hide away due to my shyness and fear of what others might say. The same with my bottoms that were almost the same shape as a thong, revealing a round ass.

I had a full body, curves and thick thighs. I looked good. And I thrived in that. Ever since I arrived this morning I had been flirting with Jax and Luca the whole time, annoying the living shit out of my brother and Santino who ended up lashing out at them for indulging me.

"Why do you care?" Santino glared at me, eyes filled with anger at someone going against his word. Jax laughed, holding my waist as I got up from his lap.

I had questioned him with a glint of mischief in my eyes. His response? No answer. But even that was clear enough. Of course, Jax being Jax had gone off on them, too. He told the two of them about how it is fine since I was no longer a kid but a full-grown adult who can make her own choices. I flipped my hair over my shoulder, letting it fall down my back where it stopped right above my ass. Heading inside the kitchen through the large terrace door, I stopped near the green chair in the corner and picked the long shawl that came with the bottoms up, tying it around my lower waist.

"It seems this new rebellious character of yours has caught quite the attention." I entered the large kitchen, the beautiful original Spanish design was kept instead of it being remodelled into something it isn't. A grand island is in the middle of the kitchen, creme walls with large cabinets, two pantries overflowing with drinks, snacks and I don't know what else. Marbled counters and high-end stove tops with large ovens. A wine cooler settled on the inside of the island and in the basement was an even larger wine room filled with different bottles from different brands and years. A whole variety. I never thought Santino was the kind of person who drinks. I had not seen him drink once since I arrived this morning and the other guys had downed shot after shot already. Or maybe he didn't wanna drink while others were around. My father was like that. He hated drinking with people and would only have some wine from mom whenever she could not finish her glass during our dinners at home. I miss those moments like nothing else.

"Hmm," I hummed a, *'is that so?'*, before turning around and jumped on top of the island. A glass of champagne in my hand that I had stolen from the basement as it was one of the very few bottles that had my attention. Not to mention, I wasn't much of a drinker of wine. It had to be sweet and not even near dry.

"I don't think it caught the right one," I spoke. "Even so, what's it to you? You hate me and could not even bother saying hello this morning and instead went right into scolding me." I glanced at Santino. His tall frame leaned against the entrance to the kitchen and garden. Eyes raking over my body, over the curve of my tits and stopped around where my thighs were. "You were the one ignoring me. You didn't even wish me a happy birthday."

"Why would I? You are the asshole here." I paused. "Or... do I have the story wrong?" I lowered my voice a bit, soft and lustful. Almost like a seductress but not quite there yet. Santino pushed his body away from the door frame and walked closer to me. Arms caging me between them. His body relaxed and yet, the full sight of him willing to fight back only kept pushing me to bite more.

I wanted to know what he looked like breaking. Whether I could chew or not whatever he would dish back, was a consequence for later. Leaning back on the counter, I used my elbows to keep me up while crossing my legs, rubbing over his thigh and near his groin teasingly. The sound of splashing around, of the music, the boys' laughter, it all became background noise.

"Shit, what sort of fuck fest is going on here?" Jax walked inside, laughing. Bad timing. I playfully rolled my eyes as I pushed Santino away from me and jumped down.

"No kind. I'm bored, I'm going to my room." Jax nods, waving at me. Santino grabs my upper arm just as I am about to walk past him. His eyes glare into my own. A large hand engulfing my upper arm, hot and thick and my mind couldn't help itself but wander towards places it shouldn't. The thought of that hand coming down on my body turned my mind into something I didn't want it to become.

Bad girl, Nova. Bad.

"Careful, muñequita. Or you might get burned." I couldn't help the slight smirk tugging at my lips. The little glint of mischief burned to life in my eyes. I want this bastard on his knees for me so badly I nearly choke on the desire. I look away for a moment. Something tells me not to start any trouble. However, something else tells me that it might end up just like how I want it.

I look back at him. Sure of myself as I speak up with a steady voice.

"What if I want to get burned, huh? What if I'm looking for that?"

Chapter 2

I walked over to my room, my lingering gaze and fast beating heart no longer the center of my attention. I had gone into the bathroom attached to my room, stripped off my bikini and jumped into the shower.

Fucking Santino. The memory of him acting like he was my boss and had all the power over me made me fume from how angry I was. How dare he try to control me! What a piece of—

I stopped my thoughts. I hate him. And yet, the sight of him half naked, looking like a god roamed my mind and turned my body on like a heater. His body heat as he stood above me on the kitchen island had my face turning red. Just that turned me into a puddle. There is no saying what I might become if he tried anything more. I never denied that there was or is some sort of attraction for him from me. By accident, I had spotted a picture with his file on Chase's desk years ago, I developed a stupid little crush on the image of Santino. That only turned to ashes when I finally met him in real life. One would think that it couldn't bloom into anything more afterwards. How wrong I was. Santino scolding me had reminded me I was far younger than him and that he saw me as a kid and nothing else. My crush was only from my side of the story, he had no feelings whatsoever.

"You are a kid! What possessed you to even think about doing such a job?!"

"Stupid heart, dumb fucked up mind." Yet I still touched myself to the thought of him. Then... and even now.

My hands follow each drop of water. Moving over the curve of my tits, over my thighs, my ass. My fingers pushing between my legs and between my lips. My pussy wet with need as I imagined the devil standing on his knees, watching me as I fingered myself until I came.

Each caress had become a wild dream, each thought of him as he touched me roughly becoming a burning desire that never ends. I wondered how big he was, how it would feel to have his cock ram inside me from behind.

The way he stood there at the top of the stairs this morning when we arrived in just sweats and no top. The way his wet hair clung to his face or how his swimming shorts were stuck to his thighs, the bulge in his pants evident, showing just how big he is. His tattoos and V-line... The worst part about it is that he had caught me looking not once but several times. The only time I could finally breathe somewhat was when he and the others went inside his office and were talking about something concerning one of their future missions. I spread my legs in the shower, leaning against the cold tiled wall, goosebumps erupting all over my body.

My fingers touching my clit softly, gently rubbing a finger over cunt which made me whimper at how sensitive I felt to the touch. Wet and dripping. My other hand grabbed one of my breasts, kneading it, my bottom lip getting caught under my teeth as I tried not to cry out my pleasure.

I glanced at myself in the mirror once I was done. The steam surrounded me like the haze in my mind wrapped around my brain. My cheeks were flushed red, my hair wet and clinging to my body as I breathed in and out, slightly out of breath and my bottom lip bitten raw as I tried to suppress my moans.

Failed that one by the way.

I hated myself for dreaming of a man that I wanted to hate. I was petty as fuck with other people, I cut others off without warning and yet here I was, turning into goddamn mush like some sick puppy meeting its master after hours of being left alone.

Puppy.

I was a sick puppy. A needy one. Why else would I act like a love-hung teenager after knowing their crush exists in the same world as them? I rolled my eyes at my thoughts. Once I finished cleaning myself up, I wrapped a towel around my body and walked out of the bathroom only to hit a wall. My body slams into the door behind me, my grip on the edges of the towel loosening. "Did you enjoy your shower, muñequita?" I swallowed hard. Santino stood before me, still half naked, dark eyes that made me cower back. My breath staggers, my heart slamming behind my rib cage as a fox-like grin corrupted his plump lips.

"I most definitely enjoyed the audio. Who knew you could have such dark secrets." I looked away from him, my bottom lip sucked between my teeth again only to have him pull it out by grabbing hold of my chin and cheeks, squeezing me in between them. His large hands engulfed half of my face.

"You drew blood," Santino whispered as he inched his face closer to mine while dragging my head upwards, his lips brushed against mine and a whimper left me.

A *whimper*. I was losing it.

Santino chuckled. "You must be a loud one then." He stated more to himself, yet I still heard him. "Oh, you got in." Finally, he pulled away from me as Cole walks into my room. He observed us for a moment, eyes moving up and down as if we were in some kind of danger.

Maybe I was. The way Santino looked at me, with a look of utter desire burning in those black orbs of his, it left me weak in the knees. If it weren't for my body leaning against the door, I would have plummeted to the floor. "Nova was showering, she couldn't hear you knocking. Chase panicked thinking something happened," Santino explained. I didn't dare look into his eyes. Too scared to face whatever look he may be sporting. Santino left us be as he heard the guys screaming downstairs for him so he went to check up on them. "Chase and Luca found some club thing that has some sort of after party afterwards. They are looking to get tickets, wanna come?"

"I don't want to be stuck in a car with drunk people. No offense, you, I love. The others?" I waved my hand left and right to show how much I cared for the rest followed by a scrunch of my nose. Cole laughs, playfully rolling his eyes.

"And here I thought you loved your brother. Things didn't go as planned?" He asked, concern flickering over this pretty face. I shrugged my shoulders, not wanting to talk about it. I glanced over at the now open door behind him.

"You know," He cleared his throat. "I can keep them busy for hours if you want to get back at San." I glance at Cole who seemed to enjoy messing with his boss. I know Cole is the type who enjoys putting others in their place, fucking with and annoying the living daylights out of everyone.

He is like a brother to me and he saw me in the same light. And not just because he was into men. Ever since I met Cole, he had kept an eye on me by becoming my friend in real life and on social media and hyping me up. There are things Chase had no idea about but Cole did.

"Why? Wanna make sure my brother gets drunk off his ass enough?" He looked taken aback only for that dangerous glint to vanish and change to a stoic look again.

"I don't know what you're talking about." I scoff, crossing my arms over my chest. "I am not blind. Besides, you have to know Chase isn't gay, right?" That had him smirking.

There was no way. Chase? My brother? "You are right. He is far too uptight to even think about it." I playfully slapped his chest. "You should find someone worthy of you, Cole-man." He chuckled.

"Thanks. I'm off, then. Let me know what your plans are."

As much as I loved the idea of going to a party, I didn't want to see the devil in human skin sucking faces with other bimbos or anything like that. Or my brother for that matter. So I dropped the topic on both things. It isn't long after that the guys had gotten ready and left. Chase came up to my room and told me to always have my phone on me. Glancing outside of my window once dressed in a red long cover-up made of braided fabric, I waited patiently for them to leave.

With everyone gone, I was going to enjoy some alone time next to the pool and tan some more while I had the chance. I walked downstairs into the kitchen and back outside, wandering over to the pool. I took the cover-up off and laid down with my feet in the water. The sound of echoing screams coming from the other side of the hill stopped my train of thought. I glanced at the large green field, the sound of people screaming, the running of horses. So peaceful—

"There is a ranch on the other side of the hill."

I almost screamed, falling into the pool as my body decided to run for it. Santino stood like a looming shadow over me while staring at the large walls all around his property. They stretched so far, cutting a quarter of the forest around the villa off and tying it to the land that belonged to the demon.

"They teach horseback riding every summer to tourists." Yeah, I was supposed to have joined a camp of sorts, too. Sadly, my brother chose something else when it came to how I spend my summertime. What the fuck is he doing here? Wasn't he supposed to have joined the guys? And then like a brick hitting my head, I got reminded about Cole's little tempting idea of fucking Santino over. I groaned as I leaned back over the water. For fuck sakes...

How did I miss such an important detail?!

"Why are you here?" I finally spoke up, a smidge of annoyance lacing my voice.

"You're in my house." I rolled my eyes.

"Keep rolling those eyes and you won't like the outcome of it." Is he serious? What can he do to me? I pushed myself away from the edge of the pool and went over to the fancy side steps, walking back up on the patio.

"Try something and I'll scream." That mischievous smirk and dark glint in his eyes shined bright like the damn summer sun. "Oh, I'm betting on it. And I *bet* you sound fucking erotic, too. I mean, the little show you previously decided to hide from me sounded pretty already. Had my cock getting all hard and ready to—"

"What the fuck is wrong with you?!" I cut him off. A blush crept over my face and due to the lack of make-up to hide it, it had all been on full display for him to see my reaction to those words. Santino walked closer, my hands instantly went up to keep space between us but that didn't stop him. He grabs my wrist and pulls me so close to him his breath fans over my face, lips almost touching in a kiss. *Again.*

"With me? Nothing. You are the one pretending to be a pure little virgin while you had your fingers shoved up all the way in that tight cunt of yours." He gripped my fingers between his own, spreading them as he brought his head down and sucked my fingers. Tasting the flesh. Leaving a trail of wetness behind just like how they were coated back in the bathroom with my own—

I stopped thinking.

My eyes went wide in shock. "Face it, little Nova. You are a little depraved slut who wants to be fucked. You loved toying with me today, flirting with my men, dancing around with Jax and Luca, riding that round ass all over the place. Showing your tits off." His face was so close to mine that I barely could breathe as he towers over me. His eyes glare into mine, looking for something. His teeth graze over my wrist, biting down when I didn't say anything until I moan in pain. A mark stays behind which he licks and then kisses.

"I dare you to deny it," When I felt him loosen up a bit, I managed to spring free and rushed inside the house.

"I am." For a second, it seemed my words had taken him by utter surprise. "Why do you look like that? You dared me to deny it. I don't want your limp cock."

"Fucking brat," Santino mutters something under his breath but I barely make one word out. I scoff as I roll my eyes, which seemed to have been such a bad idea. Before I know it, he grabbed me by my upper arm and bent me over the kitchen island. Santino's large palm coming down on my ass as I yelped at the sudden sting spreading over my entire body.

My legs almost buckling if it weren't for the grip he had on my wrist holding me in place. My mind had this little error moment as it didn't fully grasp what had just happened.

"Did you—Did you just—" I was baffled. No, worse. Utterly speechless.

"Ah!" I cried again as another slap kissed my ass. "Do you know how bad girls get punished?" Another spank landed on my ass. Making my eyes sting with tears. For a moment, he stops. A warm hand touching the tender flesh gently.

"Do you know what a safe word is, Nova?" A safe word? I nodded without hesitation. Too scared to go against him for some reason. My heart hammers in my chest, eyes stinging with tears and my thighs tightly clenched while my pussy is being a traitorous slut. There is so much going on, so many emotions that suddenly erupted through me.

"Good. Your safe word is black." He watches me, waiting for my defiance or for me to use it, to stop this.

"The safe word is set to keep you safe. Once you say it, this all stops. And you will address me as master or sir during this entire time." I watched his large reflection in the stove as he stood above me, watching me.

"Do you understand?" My entire body agrees before my brain does. Once again, I nod. "I'm going to need your words, my pretty little doll."

"Yes."

"Yes, what?" When I didn't answer, Santino spanks my ass so hard I cry out while kicking my leg. This one fucking hurt so badly. And yet, my pussy tingles and I find myself doing as told.

"Yes, I understand." My mouth is open as I gasp from the pain still burning my flesh. My ass cheeks are red, I can feel them and the sting from being hit one after the other made me rub my legs against each other.

"Yes, sir. I understand."

"Good girl."

Chapter 3

"Why must I even get punished?"

"Because that attitude of yours needs to be under control."
My attitude?! I felt offended not gonna lie. I had a perfect attitude, he was the problem.

"I don't need to be punished, asshole!"

Spank. This one was twice as hard and I cry out another curse without thinking. My legs struggle to stay straight.

"It is exactly something you need, doll. And the best part?
You are going to take it like the good girl you say you are in front of others. You will take every spanking I give you without complaining or whining. And once done, just like every good girl, you will thank me." His eyes are dark—so dark and filled with lust it almost made me moan. Not to mention the growing erection that is almost exploding in his pants teases my ass. With how thin the material of his summer shorts are, you could

see his cock clear as day. This turned him on, too. Fuck, he is enjoying this so fucking much. Had my little show done a number on him? That thing looks so big already, I am sure it would break anyone who took him. It would split *me* apart most definitely.

I sucked in a breath as I leaned back down on the cool counter. The marble design was a pretty sight to my eyes yet my mind was full of Santino and his cruel yet delicious punishment. My pussy is tingling and I try to keep my legs against each other so tightly. Once he comes closer, I wiggle my ass. Rubbing against him and feeling him up. Santino pulls back, my head and body bending backward as he grips me by hair right by the nape.

I cry out. Santino chuckles in my ear as he holds me bent backwards, my stomach kissing the edge of kitchen island.

"What a naughty girl. What? Is your cunt dripping from this?" His head hides into the crook of my neck, his breath tickling my ear as he speaks to me, a growl in his voice.

"Is your cunt crying for pleasure? Pleading to get fucked? To have my cock ram into it until it's filled with my cum to the brim?"

I moan. I fucking moan! His words were so... fuck! I don't know. They were so dirty and it did something to my stomach. It did a flip. But it... it felt good. Santino kissed my back, his teeth grazing my skin before biting down the sweet flesh.

"Ah..." He groans at the taste of me. "Let me take a look." I shook my head at him as he grabs my bottoms and unties the side strings, letting the fabric slip between my thighs only to catch it on time and throw them on the island beside my head. A wet spot had my eyes going wide. I felt embarrassment cover my cheeks. The very thought of him seeing my juices as he pulled the fabric away, seeing my private parts all soaked up because of this...

"It seems someone is enjoying this punishment. Do I have a masochist on my hands?" Amusement lingers in his voice.

"Ass..." Another spank meets my skin then two more on my other cheek. Each slap was hard and it came all bruising and with no forgiveness.

"Fuck!" I cry. His whole palm moved from my butt all the way down until it covers my whole pussy. The feeling of his whole hand there had me whimpering. His touch was rough and filled with a sick need.

A depraved need.

His fingers move between my pussy lips, massaging my entrance spot first. The pads of his fingers touch my clit squeezing it between two fingers as he watches me. My legs shake, my breathing shakes as I feel the pleasure building. Without waiting, two fingers drove between my wet folds and pushed inside of my aching hole. Curling and feeling my walls around, stretching me with no mercy. My head falls down, eyes rolling back as pleasure hits me. "And here I thought you might get scared like a little kitten. Instead, I am met with a drenched cunt loving the punishment."

"I..." I tried to speak but couldn't due to my loud moans.

"You? You what, my pretty little slut?" I bite my bottom lip. My juices coat his fingers, some dripped to the floor. Each stroke in and out had me squirming, pushing my behind to meet him for more. The lewd sounds fill the kitchen and make my face heat up. My pussy clenched around him, a knot tightening in my lower stomach. With his hand still gripping my own hands against my lower back and one of his legs keeping my right leg pinned against the island, there was nowhere for me to run. So I just stand here, taking it all like a good girl.

"Please..." I beg. My wet hair clings to my body, a strand sticking to my lower lip. Sadly, that plea became my end. He stops, pulls his fingers from my aching cunt and leaves me high and dry right when I was about to come. Instead, he grabbed both my ass cheeks and spreads them open, watching me.

"You have such a pretty hole. And such a cute pussy. Hmm," He growls. "If you could see what I see, pretty doll. Such pretty pink folds, dripping with need on my kitchen floor. The way it milks my fingers, begging to be fucked and filled up." He chuckled.

"You will count to five. If you stutter even once, we will go again from the start, however, each time, another spanking will be added to the count. Understand?"

"Yes," I breathed out. "Yes, sir."

"Good girl." His hand came down on my ass. "One." I count. Another one followed right after, each smack is divided on across each cheek. "Two, three," I shudder from the pain.

Smack. "Four!" I almost screamed. The sting hurt. I was so sure there were going to be bruises left behind after this. Either that or his hand printed on my skin.

Smack. "Five." The last hit was the loudest. The sound striking through the kitchen as I cried in pain. Tears falling down my cheeks this time.

"Look at that. What a piece of art." Santino looked down at me and admired his work. His other hand finally releases my wrists and my arms ached from being held in place so tightly. "You took that so well. You're such a good girl for me. Doesn't it feel better to let go of any restraint? Allowing yourself to enjoy something other than what society tells you is best?"

He was making fun of me, he had to. I bit my lip. My lower region aching with need for release. To be fucked and filled up.

"T-thank you, master." His hand came up to my chin, tapping my nose.

"Such a good girl." He paused. "Let's take care of you now," Placing my hands over his as he picks me up bridal style, I signal with my hand like a child asking for uppies over towards my bikini bottoms still on his kitchen island. However, Santino shakes his head, a smirk covering his plump lips. Walking out of the kitchen, he heads upstairs with me in his arms. The upper level is divided into two different hallways; the left one was where most of the guest bedrooms were with two extra bathrooms. The right side had the master suite with a connected bathroom as well as three main bedrooms with two bathroom. The grand suite belonged to Santino—I may or may not have snooped around. Not my fault I was left unattended in such a gorgeous house while I was still mad at the fucker. San walked inside his room to my surprise. A big room with a large king-sized bed in the middle with fancy nightstands.

A night lamp stood on each side of the bed built into the headboard. A thick headboard might I add. And something told me you could pull the top of it off and reveal some hidden gem. Now I really wanted to know what secrets might be hiding underneath it.

"Stay here, I will be right back." Santino dropped me on my stomach on the bed. The moment I dared move to sit up, I hissed from the pain shooting right up my spine and cursed a colorful word or two. From where I am sitting, I could hear that demon chuckling at my discomfort from the bathroom. His silhouette peeked into the long mirror above the double white sinks.

"Come here." He commanded. I stood up on shaky legs and wandered over to him. His hand came around the bikini top, pulling it off my body. On instinct, my hands fly to cover them which had him narrowing his eyes at me.

"Don't ever hide yourself from me," I stay quiet. My arms relaxed in the next few seconds and they fall by my side under his commanding gaze. "You should get in the tub while it's warm. I will rub an ointment on your ass once you get out. I will be on the bed if you need me." He grabs my chin and kissed the top of my head all tenderly before leaving me alone in the bathroom.

I settle down in the tub, my ass aching from the number of spankings I received. I had been given the remote to the TV inside the bathroom as well, scrolling through different channels and stopping on this show meant for kids that seemed a lot more interesting than I thought it would.

If Chase were to hear about me watching a kid's show after I laughed at him for watching a show with talking animals meant for little babies, he was going to have my head for this. I don't know how long I stood in the water. There had been several episodes of different shows by the time it started to cool off. The whole time, San was in his bedroom, on the bed, and scrolling through his phone. At one point he had taken a call in Spanish and one doesn't understand how fucking hot he sounded. During this time, he had come a few times in the room to check up on me.

Santino keeps calling me muñequita—which is something I still need to search up to see what it means.

"If you are tired, you should come out before you become a danger to yourself." I rolled my eyes.

"Watch it. Do you want a repeat of what happened an hour ago?" An hour? Just an hour? The events replayed again like a movie in my head with no stopping them. I shook my head at him. "No, no, no."

I glanced at him. "N-no, sir."

Santino walks over to me, helps me out of the tub and dried my body up. Careful not to rub over my sensitive skin and instead patted it dry softly. The towels were so freaking soft which was a wonder. Every time Chase washed towels they ended up like those sanding papers you need to finish wood with.

I giggled at my thoughts. Finish wood. Get it? No? Never mind then.

"Here," On the marbled sink, a shirt lay on to which he grabbed and helped me put it on. After I was done with he bath, he had brought me back to his bed and began rubbing an ointment over my bruised skin. I lay on my stomach, arms crossed. It was getting late by now and the soft blue sky was a hint of that. For a moment, I wondered over to the guys and what they were doing or how long they were going to be gone for.

"The others will be back late. The event is part of a show and knowing their whorish asses, they will stay back to greet the ladies."

"Like Magic Mike?" I hiss right after as he applies more creme to my wounded flesh. "It stings."

"It will be better after this. And Magic Mike?" Really? I go to explain but then shut right up. Maybe talking about hot men right after I got spanked isn't such a good idea. "Stay here and rest, I have some work to finish up." I glanced at him, pouting at the idea of being left alone.

"You have work even on your birthday? That's sad."

"Hmm, guess so. Wanna keep me company by spreading that pussy?" A blush crept over my cheeks.

Chapter 4

I don't know how long it has been since Santino left me to rest in his room. His scent wrapped around me like soft blanket, lulling me to sleep.

Getting out of bed, I stop in front of the large body mirror standing next to a chair with a thick braided woolen blanket draped over it. I examine my bruises flesh first before peaking inside of his walk-in-closet. I spot an island filled with fancy watches of brands I never once heard of before in rows underneath this glass case. On the other side of the island, are ties wrapped up around fancy boxes as well as those tie clips men wear placed on small cushions. Gold, silver, and some were red. Each engraved with his initials I assume.

Sweats, boxers, shirts and hoodies that I stole one of and placed it on the bed for me to take back to my room. That was my revenge after the punishment he gave me. My phone plays a song in the background all while I snooped around. It was too quiet for my liking so I had chosen an old playlist I began humming to.

I kept walking around, swaying my hips and dancing, singing the lyrics out loud. I moved further through the closet, prying around more until I came across something black. It was a black glass door that shifted once I pressed my hand against it. Slowly, it opens, revealing a large thick glass case from ceiling to floor with guns and blades. This is tucked away that easily? There is no way this is here.

Although the glass case is tough from how thick it feels to the touch, the idea still scared me.

I walk away from the closet, having had enough of looking around. I felt bad for some reason now. That conscious thing working. What if San gets mad at me for looking where I shouldn't?

With the hoodie in one hand, I sneaked out and walked down the hallway back to my room. The window is slightly open and the soft evening breeze filters through. The soft scent of flowers from the hill behind the house has cleared the room from any other scent that was of the guys and I took a big whiff of it.

It was soft and clean and I wondered if I could get to the hill and pluck some of the flowers for my room. My phone goes off suddenly, bringing me back to reality as I thought about the flowers. Chase's picture of him dressed in a panda onesie for Halloween last year, appear on my screen. He had been asked by one of his friend's children to wear one and match with him while they went trick or treating.

"What's up?" I ask, a bored tone greeting him.

"Did you know, that if you get laid once in this lifetime, you might be less rigid?" I want to roll my eyes at that, yet instead, I choose to ask him again what he wants "Get to the point."

"The guys and I are heading to an after-party once the show is done. It should be one more hour before we leave."

"And... what does that have to do with me?" He sighs on the other side of the line. Chase was the kind to *not* get to the point at all. I love my brother but sometimes he is too much even for me as his sister. "Chase."

He clears his throat. "Just checking in, ok? Has Santino been bothering you? Giving you a hard time?" My eyes went wide. I picked the shirt up from over my behind and watched my ass once more. My pussy clenches at the memories of him spanking me, spreading my pussy lips apart and watching me drip with need for him once he was done punishing me.

"All good. Come on, he can only try something. I will have him begging for forgiveness in no time!" Chase laughs.

"Yeah, yeah. I am sure. You can make anyone beg for forgiveness with how fast you can annoy a person." I fake gasped.

"I am not as bad as you say I am."

"Never denied it. You can, however, fuck a person up if you want. Remember Callum? In high school?"

"He had it coming. I warned him to leave me alone yet he didn't wanna listen. Not my fault."

"Whatever. Hey, listen. Give word to Santino about something. I called the fucker several times but he isn't answering. Tell him to check his work phone and call Viper back." I stayed quiet for a moment.

"Viper?" I raised an eyebrow as I stared at myself in the mirror. That name was previously mentioned a few times, just enough for me to develop a pure hatred for this dude. On the other line, my brother stayed quiet for a second, the sound of music and wolf-whistles echoes in my ear as Chase decides to break the silence by humming a yes and continues speaking.

"I know what you think. But Viper is a good boss. He knows things not even Santino can get his hands on."

"I thought Santino was your boss." I pique. "San is our group's leader. His boss is Viper. The big boss." I sigh, letting it go.

"Fine."

With that, I end the call and toss my phone on the bed. A groan fills the room as I get up and head downstairs. San's office was set beside the staircase, down another hallway. The walls are filled with paintings of landscapes costing thousands of dollars if not more. Some of the names were classic ones I knew well. Painters I adored and took as my inspiration. If there was no painting, then there were these big vases made of this golden-like material. Although from how dull it looks, it feels more like copper than gold.

Stopping before a double set of brown wooden doors, I softly knocked on it and enter once a voice welcomes me in.

"Muñequita." I tilt my head at the sound of that nickname. "What does that mean? I keep forgetting to look it up." He smirks. "Wanna find out on your own?" I shake my head. "Tell me."

"So demanding. Who is the master here? Me or you?" His eyes darken as they land on me. Lust fills those beautiful orbs of his.

"Y-you are." Santino pushes his chair slightly away from the desk and extends his arm out, waiting for me to come closer and take it. I placed my hand into his and his large palm wraps around my slim fingers. Muscles and veins flexing beneath my own skin as I touch him.

"My brother called." I began, looking around at the same time. A large bookshelf lay on the other side of the room in this pushed-back design. The wall is divided into two pieces. The first half is the bookshelf that seemed to be built into it while the other side has a huge TV portraying lots of small screens.

Each presenting a certain room in this house.

Stalker much. I almost laugh at my thoughts. Santino would be a good stalker I won't lie. His nickname during his work is *Shadow*. The first time I heard it, I pictured Santino dressed like batman almost, minus those bat ears batman has on his head and jumping building to building. "Hm, is that it?" I shake my head. His office is covered in papers piled in a short stack beside his right arm, a simple black laptop as well as his personal phone and work phone. "He told me to tell you to call Viper back." My tone most definitely tells him how I fell about Viper. San chuckles as he stares at me. Glancing back over to the TV, I watch each little screen and spot his own bedroom as well as mine.

Frozen.

On *me!*

Oh my god! My cheeks turn a bright red as I spot myself taking a picture in the mirror of his closet. I was sitting down before it, my ass between my legs, shirt ridden up and my face covered by my phone while I snapped a pic to keep as memory.

The fucking demon grins as he watches me. Fine, if he wants to go down like this, I can play games, too.

With a teasing smile, I glanced at him. "It seems someone enjoys watching. Got a voyeurism kink I should know about?" I step between his legs as I push my body over his. Santino tilts his head to one side, observing me with a shining desire in his eyes as I settle on his lap. His dick answers that question before he does.

"What if I do?"

I bite my lower lip, the idea turns me on. His arms shoot out, wrapping them around my waist and hoisting me up on the desk a second later. "Take your shirt off." He commands me. Tone rough, thick with need. "What?"

"You heard me, take your shirt off. Show yourself to me." Mischief bursts into his eyes. He is having so much fun. I know he is expecting me to deny him, to fight and rebel like today by the pool. Instead, I do as he wants. I move my hands over my body teasingly slow and agonizingly sweet all while I stare into his eyes, holding our gazes locked on each other. The shirt vanishes from my body and I let it drop to the ground beside his feet. My breasts in full view for him to enjoy. This time I wasn't feeling self-conscious like back in his bathroom.

"Fuck..." He groans. The sight of him watching me, knowing that these sounds came because of me have me weak in the knees.

"Do you know how gorgeous you look, doll face? Following your master's commands." He moves closer, hands moving beneath my breasts as he pushes them up and sucks on one of them. My head falls back, pleasure rushing. "Is that what it means? I thought it meant pretty doll or whatever you called me earlier. Hmm."

He shook his head. "Muñequita means little doll. Because you barely are five-six. If that's what you mean." I nod and giggle. "I'm not barely. I am five foot—" I wanted to lie but thought about the consequences. If he hates the brat he would hate the liar, too. His lips pull up in a grin on his delicious lips. He ran his tongue over me as he pulls away from my breasts.

Santino looks ready to eat me and I am tickling at the idea of him having his fill of me. I bring my hands over my body, massaging my tits before leaning slightly back and raising my leg on the table, spreading them.

"Fuck." He groans. Santino stares with so much hunger at me it has my entire body catching fire. My core burns with desire and it drives me utterly insane. His touch has me craving more and more of him. My hatred seems to turn into ashes and it is reborn as a desire. A sinful one. This has to be a sin from how badly I wanted him to ruin me.

"Already wet, doll face? What a needy little slut you are." I bite my lower lip, agreeing with him.

"Spread your legs." He commands. The second I spread my legs wider, a cold chill runs down my spine. My lower body almost humps the air, looking for some sort of relief.

"Do you need to come, baby?" I nod. "Show me how much you need it. Play with yourself." I lower my gaze for a second, not sure what to do. I never had someone watch me masturbate—never mind tell me to play with myself.

Santino sees me hesitating, he leans forward just enough to come closer to me but not to touch me with his body. His hand wraps around my own, engulfing it whole and drives two fingers deep inside me.

I gasp.

"You act as if you have never touched yourself. Shall I remind you of your play earlier today? How my name sounded coming from your lips while you made yourself come?"

His fingers together with my own push inside. of me with no patience. Curling and pumping in and out, smearing my wetness over my fingers to the connecting points with my palm, stretching me wide. Santino let's go of me a moment later, settles back down in his chair and watches my pussy with a sinful lust. The next moment, he brings his hand up to his lips and licks my juices from his knuckles all the way up to his finger tips. I stay like that, mouth slightly open and cheeks red. I move my finger slightly out only to push it back in, doing exactly what he taught me to do moments ago until I can feel my walls tightening around them.

Leaning back on my other hand, I pull my fingers away and bring them up to my mouth, tasting myself as well all while watching Santino the whole time. His eyes are everywhere while mine are on his and his growing erection in his pants. I almost laugh, it is amusing to see the type of reaction I am having on him.

And I can't help the drive I get§ to do more to him. Bringing my hand back over my clit, I started moving in gentle circles, the sensation making my hips buckle on the desk and whimper at the pleasure I get.

"So you are into voyeurism after all." I smirk.

"Never denied it, muñequita."

Chapter 5

Santino's hand caresses my thighs, pushing his thumb into my skin, nodding in approval at every reaction he coaxes out of me. He kisses my skin, every inch is covered in these soft, petal-like kisses that turn into bruises and bite marks that leave my brain numb and my pussy begging to be fucked.

"Hmm," He moans into my flesh, moving closer and closer to my clit. Hands grip my waist as he pins me in place. My back arches into his touch, needing to feel him more, needing to get rid of that pressure, of this ache. Santino moves one hand gently over my pussy all while grinning at my desperation.

A chuckle erupts from him as he stares at me with lust filled eyes. I move my lower body against his, earning a slap over my clit, making me cry from the sting.

"You get your cunt fucked when I want. Cry as much as you want and you won't be getting off."

"How cruel." I whimper.

"Cruel? Cruel is me fingering this cunt until you black out from stopping just when you are about to come. Cruel is me ramming my cock so deep in you and using it as my personal little fuck toy, my cum dumpster and not letting you get your release not even once, baby." His eyes are dark, his breathing ragged as he stands up from the chair and leans over my naked body. My legs are forced up, pushed back and against the table, exposing me fully.

"What a little whore you are," He grins. "Look at this pretty pussy dripping on my desk. Tell me, doll face. Does it feel good to be spread open like so? To be watched when you're most vulnerable and can't do anything about it? To be stripped of your power and fucked like the whore you are?" The way he speaks to me had me losing my mind. I whimpered as I nodded.

Santino is fucking insane. The way he demands things and keeps control over me, the way he takes whatever he desires. This is different from the other times I had slept with my ex. Those times were boring and he would make himself cum and be done with it. I don't think I even came once during our time together.

I sucked in my bottom lip. I can't handle it anymore.

"You're gonna be a good girl, won't you? You will take everything I give you and thank me for it, right?" I bobbed my head up and down while staring at him. Despite the way he handles me with roughness and little to no mercy, I felt safe.

His eyes search mine for any fear, his hand touching my jaw, running up and down my cheek and over my bottom lip as he pulls it free before pushing his thumb in my mouth.

"You remember your safe word?"

I stop sucking his thumb. "Yes, sir," I answer just like he taught me. Santino brings his lips over my breasts, grabbing the tender buds and biting them, pulling. My nipples harden from the pain and when he pulls back, he blows cold air over them. My head falls back abasing the desk, my moans fill the office. I can feel myself becoming wetter with each game.

"Fuck—please…" I begged.

"Already begging?"

"Please, I need you."

Santino pushes his lips slightly out in that thinking position while looking up at the ceiling. Thinking whether to torture me or give in and fuck me just like how I needed. His body seems so relaxed to everything. How does he have so much control over himself? I am dripping with need and here he is, laughing at my deplorable state.

"Is that so?" I nod quickly. Making a move with my hand to grab his own but fail. "What a messed up little thing you are. Is your cunt aching for me?" I moan a yes as he shoves two fingers inside me and starts pumping in and out.

"Hmm, I don't believe you." I plead through my cries as he traces a finger over my clit and rubs it left and right teasingly. "Prove to me how badly you need it, how badly you need me." I glance up.

"Get on your knees."

On my knees? Santino leaned back on his chair as he settles down. His smug face has this sure of himself look that says I won't pull through on his demand. For some reason, in my mind, Santino acts as if he is trying to push me away through each action he takes. Rough, demanding, the safe word, the punishments. I never knew he was a dom.

Then again, there is little I knew about him.

I lock my gaze on him, a smug smile growing on my own lips. Gently, I place my legs back down, sliding off of the table and drop down before his chair where I settle myself between his legs. I move my hands upwards, touching his legs and dragging my palms up over his shorts until they land on the bulge pushing against the thin fabric.

The sight of Santino's friend in my view made me gasp as it jumped up. His cock is huge and I am sure it's going to rip me apart. It felt overwhelming against my core moments ago but never mind seeing it with my own eyes.

He is big. Of course, he is. San is a fucking giant.

Sitting on my knees, looking up at him through my wet lashes, I feel my heart hammering in my chest like crazy. His hand comes down under my chin, cupping it gently as he drags my head up. Dark eyes looking into my soul, looking for something that tells him I want to run away.

"Shit. What a fucking slut you are. Does your brother know the type of perverted things going through that mind? Hmm?

Or how you love being fucked by someone so much older than you?" I pout. "You aren't that old."

"I am. To someone who is sane, I am. But you enjoy it, got some issues we should talk about?"

I giggle. "Got a daddy kink *I* should know about? First the watching, the spanking, the good girl nickname—"

"Careful, doll face. You are my pretty little fuck toy. *Mine.* I own you, not the other way around." There os no waiting, no being gentle, no softness or anything like that with Santino. He wants me in every deprived way. He wants me bonded to him in every bruising way he can come up with. And fuck I was so fucking ok with that. Santino grabs his cock and slaps my mouth with it like a lollipop while I stick my tongue out for more. Just like Christmas lights, my eyes light up.

"It won't fit." My words down on me. Realizing how big he is and how unprepared I am. Chuckling, he shakes his head.

"Hmm, it might not. But aren't you the one who said you would be ok with getting burned? This is your chance, muñequita." He tucks my hair behind my ear. Rubbing my thighs against each other to get some sort of friction going on had done nothing to my aching cunt. Santino sees this. His hand grips my hair tightly from the lower back and drags me up on my knees.

"Naughty girl. What? Are you dripping on my floor?" I try speaking, however, whimpers and cries cut me off followed by his mouth hungrily slamming onto mine. I can't help but moan in his mouth making him swallow the sound right up. My hands wrap around his neck as I opened my mouth for him. His lips taste like mint, his tongue darting out and forcing itself into my own. Exploring every inch of it and leaving behind a soft spicy taste that I want more of. Bent over my own body, his dick touches my chest and I gasp as he continues kissing me. My hand ventures down to it, grabbing his cock and squeezing it. Feeling the tip with the pre-cum, touching the veins that are pulsating against the pads of my fingers.

"Hmm. Fuck." I grin into our heavy make-out session. He is already dripping from how hard he is. Santino pulls away from me, standing back straight as I kept playing with his dick. Thick veins, pre-cum and the sight of pleasure written all over his face gave me the confidence to keep going.

I stick my tongue out, touching the tip where a rod is pierced right through the head. Two balls on each side. I flick my tongue softly over the tip, sucking it like I would a piece of candy. I kiss down the length of it all while rubbing the base with one hand and keeping myself steady with the other by having it lay over his lap.

"My little toy. Where did you learn these tricks from, huh?" His voice is riddled with pleasure. His hand pushes through my hair and pulls it out of my face to be able to watch me better. A look that tells me dirty secrets and dark desires he keeps hidden ready to use them on me, crosses his features. Santino uses the grip on my hair as leverage over my head and mouth, guiding me further down on his cock, pushing himself so far down my throat I start gagging and coughing. Spit drips down the sides of my mouth. "You have cute tricks. But you ain't a pro yet, baby." He mocks. "Shall I make you a pro, doll face?" Make me a pro at sucking cock? Or just *his*?

"You are just big. I've... practiced." I mutter out of breath.

"Is that so?" I hum a yes while taking a deep breath as he pulls me up for air again.

"On what did you practice, do tell? On other dicks?" Just as he speaks, the image of me on someone else runs through his mind. I can feel the anger through his grin on the back of my head, though it's harsh. It's not painful enough to make me scared. It's more of a pressure, a small threat of sorts. Santino is jealous and fuck he looks gorgeous right now. And how perfect this is. Finally, something has presented itself to me. A small weak point he never shows that I can now use against him.

"Blake. A friend. An ex better yet. He allows me to practice on him." His eyes turn even darker if that is possible. With no remorse or gentleness, he has his cock back in my mouth, forcing it as far down as he can. The taste of his cum dripping down my tongue made me moan as he exploded all over my tongue. I go to swallow of it and grin as I show him what I did. The pain mixed with the wicked hold had me clenching my thighs. I am aching with need, my juices leaking and coating the ground to the point I thought I was going to come just form this.

"What a little slut I got on my hands." Santino pulls me up from the ground and on his lap. His dick touches my core and I rub myself on him, loving the feeling. "Please..." I beg again. Yet my plea is met with a mere laugh. San pushes me back on the table, spreading my legs wide open before bringing his mouth down on my clit and started biting, sucking and fucking me with his tongue. The sudden wave of pleasure had me squealing. I arched my back from the sweet feeling that hit me all of a sudden, my hands coming down on his head as I try to push him away.

His hands however, grab mine and pins them down over my stomach, one holds them there while the other pushes my left leg down against my side and table, spreading me as much as he can.

"Hm... shit! So fucking delicious." Gasps and cries echo. "Ah, that feels so good!" My words are slurred. At this point it's a battle of words and cries pleasures.

"Please, I can't—" The way he sweeps his tongue over my clit, it is something different for me. I was so sensitive from being teased the whole day by him that now it's all too much. His tongue pushes inside, tracing every corner and tasting every part of me. His fingers follow his tongue.

One.

Two fingers.

Three. They stretched me out so much it fucking hurts so good...

"I think—Oh god, I'm gonna cum!"

"Good. Come for me, scream my name. Tell the world who is fucking you right now."

"Fuck, San... Santino!" I bite my lip as a round of shudders blows through my spine and has me crying. My stomach is in knots and once that feeling erupts, I am nothing but a shaking mess with a numb mind.

"So perfect." Santino cups my chin, kissing my lips and having me taste myself on his lips and tongue.

"Thank you, master."

"Oh no, baby. I'm not done with you yet, my pretty little doll."

Chapter 6

"Keep your hands above you." I do as told. In one swoop, my legs reached over the table, spreading me again for him while the tip of his cock teases my entrance. His cock moves in me after slapping my pussy with the tip. My slick folds make it easier for him to fuck me.

"Hmm, yes…" My voice is quiet as tears form in my eyes. I knew it, he is going to split me and he barely is inside me.

"Try to relax."

"Fuck, easy to say when you aren't the one—" I stop as he moved deeper.

"S–San…hmm, wait, please. Fuck." He stays put, not moving, not demanding. He is waiting for me, staring down at me while my hands were gripping the edge of the desk and moved to hold his, my pussy grips his cock in place so tightly I thought I might strangle it.

However, he doesn't mind. He only groans. Leaning forward over my body, he sweeps my hair out of the way as his mouth kisses my shoulder blade softly before moving over to the other one and then down to my breasts. "You are such a good girl for me. You are doing so well taking me. What a good little slut. Breathe, baby. I got you" I gasped. A shudder rippled through me as each sweet word filled my head.

Huh, look at that. Degradation and praise kink mixed in the same fucking bowl. Could I be any more desperate? Do not answer that. P

lease don't.

Santino moves again once I calmed down, he waited for me to adjust and once I was ready, he pulls out of me before slamming his cock back. "So tight, so delicious." He mutters, head falling back as pleasure consumes us both.

The sound of people coming from over the hill had me freezing in place which made Santino chuckle at my desperate attempt to sort of hide myself just in case. The office layout had this large window staring right into the hill. He pulled me all of a sudden up by my wrist, turns me around and places me on his lap while he leans back against the chair and turns us around to face the large window. Walls surround the garden, yet they weren't tall enough to hide it or the pool. On the opposite side, the walls are tall and made of wooden pallets covered inverted vines and flowers. The one looking over the hill is nothing but a fence made of round wooden posts.

In the distance, you can spot the riders on horses making their way back to the ranch. My entire body turns red as a ripe tomato. The fucker laughs behind me, a full healthy laugh. He hoists me up, arms beneath my legs.

"Shy about them seeing this pussy being ruined?" Santino moves his hips, ramming his cock all the way in. I gasp from the feeling of being full so fast. The piercing he has tickles my insides and I feel so fucking good.

"Do you think they can see you? Just imagining them watching my cock going in and out of this tight cunt of yours gets me even harder, baby." I cam feel it getting bigger as he moves in and out with force.

"I wonder what they might think? Would they think about what kind of a slut you are? A pretty whore who enjoys being watched? Hmm? What do you think? Seeing you naked, tits out, covered in my marks." He pauses while biting down on my neck, sucking the skin and bruising it. My hips move on their own as I whimper.

"Or maybe, just maybe. They might think that they could also have a go at fucking this pretty cunt." I gasp as Santino plunges his cock as deep as he cam go in one hard stroke. Jealousy striking him. "No. No, no, no. You are mine. They can watch if I allow them. But you are mine. Only I get to fuck you, to own you. To taste you." My mind is turning numb, my legs aching from how he holds them up, keeping me spread. I look up, just enough to be able to see my own reflection in the window. I try speaking, try using full words only to fail badly. "Tell me, baby. Whose are you?"

"I…" Incoherent words that turn into moans. He hums a response as he fucked me. The chair scrapes abasing the floor, hitting the desk behind us. The sound of skin against skin kissing echoes through the room and it's fucking delicious.

"I'm your pretty slut." I speak through ragged breaths and numb mind. "Indeed. My fuck toy, my pretty hole to use and fill all the way up to the brim with my seed." San pushes me over the table again, this time face down. My hands tied behind my back as he takes me rougher and harder. Slamming his cock deeper and deeper, moving even the table with how much force he was using. My body began to ache and the only sound coming from me were lewd moans and cries that die in my throat as the very breath is being fucked out of me.

Shudders and my stupid begging for more pleases him and I can hear it. But best of all, I can feel it.

"Only one person can fuck you like this. Tell me, who can fuck you like this? Who can make you cum and fill this hole?" A hand comes down hard over my ass, painting the skin red. My breath catches in my throat as I try to focus on what he was saying. My stomach is in tight knots and my mind is numb as shit from how close to coming I am.

"Yo—you can."

"What's my name, doll face."

"San—Santino."

"Say it again."

I cry, my stomach tightens, a tingling sensation has me screaming his name over and over again.

"Santino! Fuck, yes!" His hand holds my throat, bending me backwards and cutting my air supply off just enough to see black spots as he fucks me from behind until I am a liquid mess in his hold.

"What a pretty mess." The second I come, San is right behind me, filling me with his seed just like he said he would.

***

The TV plays an old show I had found in the wide collections of DVD players. I didn't think they still made these things. Or that Santino was someone who enjoyed collecting them. Speaking of, San is in the kitchen preparing food for us. Chase had called me again not five minutes ago for a check-in. I am also very, super-duper sure he is drunk off of his ass.

Thankfully Cole is the sane one in the group and was keeping a good eye on them. This also meant that I may or may not have a full picture collection of drunk idiots making a fool of themselves. Luca is dancing with a girl who is all drunk and looks like a penguin doing it, not to mention that Jax and my brother were so out of it that they were making out with a wooden pillar. Now these are golden pictures I could use on wedding days.

Santino asked me what was going on and once I showed him my phone, he groaned, annoyed with them. "How am I supposed to present a team full of well-behaved men who have their shit together when this is what they do when they are alone?" I glance at him with wide eyes. "Are we talking about the same people?" I question him.

"I am hoping to shape them into soldiers who can fucking represent the organization." I giggled. The way he speaks, it feels almost as if Santino is prepping them to join some sort of underground mafia world or something.

"Cole is the only one not drunk off of his ass."

Santino scoffs, shaking his head as he hands me my phone and goes back to cutting carrots into small thin strips. The way he cooks is so pretty. Clean and steady, he knows every step so perfectly that it leaves me quite shocked. Usually, I am the one who cooks since I cannot trust Chase in the kitchen with fire and a knife. Recently, both me and Chase have been thrown out of the kitchen since my brother had hired a professional chef. I placed my phone on the island and settle down on the stool, staring at Santino as he chops away.

"So..."

"So?"

I place my elbows on the table and lean my head down on my hands. "What did Chase want? He sounded a bit..." I weight my words with a head tilt as I ponder what word was best used in this case.

"Not scared per se, but something along that. Chase talked about Viper to me earlier, how he was looking for you." He nodded, not once looking at me.

"Chase told me you don't like him." I agreed. "Not denying it. Everything Viper hands Chase work wise, it always ends up with my brother either having a broken rib, wrist, ankle, almost going blind," I pause. "I can go on and on... I used to hate you just the same. That is before Chase told me that Viper is the one handing these cases out most of the time." I sigh.

I was mad not gonna lie. I hated this line of work. Then again, Chase picked it because it paid fucking well. He didn't get to finish school, didn't get to graduate and go to university, chase his dreams or things like that. After our parents vanished, he was forced to cut his growing up and become a parent.

He had to take care of me. At the time, I was fourteen, and I needed a parent to grow up well—or, as our aunt and uncle phrased it, I needed a parent to grow up *well*. I barely knew them and since Chase had just turned eighteen, he had full rights over my custody since he was the first in line. I knew I sort of ruined his life, all his girlfriends ended up leaving and it almost always was after they met me and learned about our story. I felt bad, thinking I ruined his life despite him always reassuring me that it isn't so. Chase was given this job through a friend of our dad's after hearing what happened to us. He had heard how skilled Chase is with computers and had immediately told one of his friends about my brother.

And so, someone took a chance on him. Which made Chase accept instantly. Never once has he looked back since then. His goal was to see me grow up well, in a good warm house, studying and achieving my goals when he couldn't. This job, it gives him a thrill and keeps him on his toes. I miss him most of the time since we barely hang out now with his missions becoming a lot longer and rougher than the ones before, especially now with a full team. Which is why I hate Viper so much. Next to the fact that these outings are fucking dangerous, it always makes me extremely aware of how fast and easily someone's life could be taken.

"I am scared he might not come back one day. I only have him as my family."

"What about your dad's brothers? Or your mother? Does she have siblings?" I roll my eyes at the mention of their names.

"Assholes and utter shitheads. My dad's eldest brother had gone down a rabbit hole of gambling and lost all the money he inherited from his grandfather. So I have no idea where he is. The youngest is the fucker that I cannot stand. He tried to get custody of me since I had not inherited my inheritance yet. Wanted to use me for his gain since he was taken out of grand-pa's will." Family issues at their finest. "I didn't grow up poor, not even before. And thanks to Chase, I was able to live my lavish life further. However, I rather be poor and know my brother is safe and sound than having to worry every fucking second of my life, thinking, 'What if this is the last time I see him?'" Santino listens as I ramble on.

"My mother has only one sister but I never met her. The only thing I know is that they grew apart long before my mom turned eighteen and it has been what? Over twenty five years or something?" I questioned myself more then him.

"Other than that. I have no one."

Santino stops chopping the veggies and grips my chin over the kitchen island. "I promise Chase won't fuck his life over. Despite being a total nut job and making out with a pillar, he is very smart. Chase and Jax are my left and right hand." Before Santino can continue talking, someone cuts him off by laughing and applauding. For a slip second, I think it's the guys.

A tall figure steps inside the kitchen, dressed in black from head to toe. Pants, a fancy shirt unbuttoned and revealing tattoos, not to mention these leather straps wrapped around his body—over his shoulders, around his chest and waist. A gun at his side and matching leather short gloves. I stare at him, deep dark green eyes that are locked on me, his gaze trailing over my naked legs making me completely aware of what I was wearing. And how naked I am.

"Sweet to know ya made friends with lunatics, San. Then again, ya always had a death wish coming." His voice is rough and thick. He sounds Russian but with a softer edge.

"Viper, nice to see you too." He chuckles. This is Viper? He is a complete shadow of a man. A void of a person since even his hair is so fucking dark. Or maybe it's the light? It was getting rather late by now, somewhere around seven maybe eight-ish? I glance between the two of them.

"And who is this pretty thing?" He steps forward, coming closer and grabs hold of my chin between his thumb and pointer finger. I pull my head away from him harshly and glare at Santino. The fucker is only grinning at me. He was enjoying this.

"This is doll face. Can you see why?" Santino leans down, his eyes watching me, staring into my soul and daring me to act out. This would be the perfect opportunity for him to punish me if I acted out, if I rebelled.

"Fuck yeah. She reminds me of one of those plastic sex dolls with working holes I can fuck." Viper picks a thick chunk of my hair from my shoulder and pulls at it. I have a hatred for Viper that runs deeper than my little high school frustration with Santino from before. "You can fill her with cum to the brim, too. Very grateful afterward."

"Is that so? Have you fucked her pussy yet?" A gasp leaves me as I hear them talking. "I have. A tight pretty pink hole."

"Enough! I am not some slut or whore you can bad mouth." Santino walks around and over to me before slamming his lips onto mine. It's not sweet, but possessive and comes with a warning, it's clashing of teeth and bruised lips. One hand comes around my waist while the other pulls my shirt up and reveals my ass, my back faces Viper. His hand spanks my ass red once again only to kneed it afterwards.

"You are not. I apologize. And so does Viper." The fucker nods. A fake look of guilt on both of their faces as he kept staring at me. Mischief hiding in his dark green eyes. "Viper and I have some work to do in the office. Put some food on a plate and drink water. No sugary drinks or alcohol." I roll my eyes as I walk past him and over to the stove.

"Roll those eyes again and I won't hesitate to break that tight little cunt of yours, baby. I'm not ashamed of making Viper witness you breaking for me while begging for more." My eyes go wide as I stand frozen in place. From the corner of my eyes, Viper checks me out. A smirk on his lips as he leans against the wall with crossed arms. That idea makes me shudder. My bottom lip finds itself sucked up by my upper teeth as I stare at Santino. He would make true of his words. He would spread me open, spank me, have me crying and everything else in between. And the idea of it? It made me drip.

San chuckles in my ear. "It seems you enjoy the idea of voyeurism a lot more then you think, doll face. Or is it the thought of hate fucking that makes your pussy wet?" He pushes with one slap across my ass before leaving me alone in the kitchen.

Chapter 7

After dinner, I settled down on my bed once I changed into a pair of silky blush pink pajama set with lace around the edges and chest area. Santino and Viper are inside his office, chatting and plotting world domination most likely. I couldn't get the image of Viper and Santino out of my head. The image of them followed by their words and how they spoke of me had left me breathless and I am so mad at myself and my body for the way it reacted like I was some sort of actual sex doll built for their pleasure and only theirs.

"Fuck yeah. She reminds me of one of those plastic sex dolls with working holes I can fuck." Viper, that fucker...

The way Santino took care of me made me feel safe. Yet, whatever that was, had me burning with a thrill and left me questioning myself so badly that I wanted to storm into his office and demand answers from him. But what would he say?

Both of them would laugh right in my face. Questioning me and what I enjoyed rather than give me answers.

Or do you want to see if Santino would follow through with his threat? Shut up brain! I am so doomed. This never happened before. Never had I questioned my desires or sexuality or anything of the sorts and here are these two fucking assholes turning my whole self upside down. I grab my phone and start scrolling through social media as much as I could.

I watched a hot biker cook, stared at a sexy model and found some new books to add to my never-ending list of unread books for when I get back home. I also decide to type out a drafted idea for my winter art project, which we have every year as part of the art course I took. Each art student must participate in a contest of any kind, depending on their major. You get grades from it, and it also counts as part of your end of year exam.

I was thinking of doing a winter oil painting. I had come across the old story of the girl with the matches, and the scene I imagined felt perfect since it would be winter when we had to present our piece in front of a jury. I text some of my friends with the idea and every single one of them gives me heart emojis. I ask them how they are doing and one of them sends a crying emoji after another.

Sasha: I love Russia, but this is chaos. Someone help me.

Rosalie: Tell me about it. France is fun, but I have been here so many times. I love my mother but can we like, visit other places, too? *Insert eye roll emoji.*

Sasha: I am so fucking thankful I have my sweet sisters-in-law here. I would die otherwise with those brothers of mine. *Insert laughing emoji.* *Insert death skull emoji*

I rolled my eyes at the texts coming in, shaking my head at these two.

I was so bored that at one point, I must have fallen asleep without even realizing it.

The soft touch of something moving between my legs had me stirring in my sleep. I groan in annoyance, move my legs up and kick whatever it was. Something grabs my ankles, pulling them back down and pinning them in place. A wave of cold air tickles my back, the shirt rides up and warm rough hands grabbed my skin with no gentleness to it.

"So soft…" A murmur, a voice so soft I barely hear it in my hand asleep state. I try opening my eyes, yet it feels like something is keeping them shut.

Whatever it is, it vanishes just as fast as it came. The touches are gone and I fall back asleep in a snap of a finger.

When I wake up again, it is fully dark outside with no sign of anyone around. I glance around me and spot the window to the little balcony wide open, the night air sweeps in and making me shiver. I drag a hand over the spot next to me, for some reason I hoped to find San or my phone but came across nothing and no one.

Speaking of phones, mine is no longer beside me. Like how Velma used to search for her glasses, I start feeling around the bed for the damn thing. Once I spot it on the nightstand, face down and— and battery fucking dead. Of course. Fucking fantastic. "Fuck this…" I mutter.

Plugging it in, I wait for the battery sign to pop up. "What the?" There is no electricity? Really? A house this big and fancy and Santino doesn't pay the bill for that? Something crawled up my spine and fear tugs at every corner. What if something happened? What if Viper did something? I tap my chest where my heart is and try to breathe, calming my mind first. Jumping to conclusions from just this isn't a good idea. First things first, find Santino. And then figure the rest out.

Still, to just try it, I grab the lamp on the other nightstand and try turning it on. Nothing. Everything is down.

Grabbing the courage I could find, I open the door and call out into the hallway for San.

Silence and the soft echo of the empty hallway is all that greets me. I call out once, twice, each time getting closer to the staircase until I am at the bottom, standing in the hallway leading to his office. I peek into the kitchen first only to be met with utter silence. Everything cleaned up, I had done the dishes but the hot pot had been left on the stove and now that too, was put away. Looking down the dark hall, the paintings look more alive now as I made my way to Santino's office. There is no noise coming from inside and once I stand fully before the door, I push the it wide open and enter.

There is…no one?

The place is empty, no sign of the two of them at all. Across the desk, there are scattered papers and a note pinned to the window behind it the table which has be blushing for a second, remembering what happened in this room. I pick the note up and read the beautiful writing on it.

"Let's play a game of cat and mouse. Whoever finds who first, wins. The loser gets to be punished by the other. Are you up for the challenge, doll face?" The words are written in sharpie and I want to scowl at how perfect his writing is.

"Cursive. The fucker knows cursive while I struggle with it?" Life was truly unfair sometimes. I continue reading.

"You have free rein in looking inside the forest. Be careful, though. There are secrets lurking about, little sex doll."

I can practically feel Santino smirking through this paper. The other note… it felt like a threat. *Little sex doll.* The forest? Fuck… It looks like a spot straight out of a horror movie and I am the first victim to die. My heart thrashes in my chest, my head feels dizzy and my entire lower side is doing flips. I push my thighs shut, afraid of the answer my body is giving me.

A game.

Santino wants to play a game? I am sure I can play along. Maybe toss some mayhem of my own into the mix. I have to find him, right? Simple. Yet the issue is that the fucker knows the forest like the back of his hand since it's part of his land.

That is my only issue here. That, or he could hide in the shed he told us to stay away from. Curiosity got the best of me right now, though. I stare into the open field on the left of. On the other side, the forest begins to spread over the small stone fence that barely reaches knee length. There is no movement except for the soft dance of branches. The open field is empty of people, no sound coming from the ranch on the other side either. There is only pure silence. And that silence sends chills down my spine like nothing else.

The thought of being the one who punishes Santino, tying him up, teasing him, running my fingers over his smooth tatted skin while I bite and leave my mark on him the same way he did me has me dancing with excitement.

"Fuck this... " I glance around me. This was his plan. He cut the electricity off to fuck with me, to toy with my mind and have me already fearing him. To fear his stalking, his insanity for these mad games. He is trying to drive me insane with all of this, to make me run away. I glance one more time outside into the distance before turning around and going back upstairs to grab some shoes and tossed them on, not caring that I was going out in a pair of pajama shorts and a cropped top.

The little spaghetti straps doing nothing to keep me warm. Excitement rushes through me and heats my body up enough, though.

No phone, no sanity left and full on curiosity.

"Careful, muñequita. Or you might get burned."

The words from this morning echoes in my head again so loud it feels like they are being spoken in my ear.

"What if I want to get burned, huh? What if I'm looking for that?"

Chapter 8

The forest.

The second I step over the little fence I can feel every moving thing follow me down the path that ends up cut of out of nowhere. Branches, and a large thick tree trunk that is ripped at the roots and left on the ground.

Branches, green leaves and no light whatsoever. I can feel the hair on my back stand up with how eery all of this feels. My entire body is on high alert and for a moment, I think I am going to faint from how long I kept my breath in. There is no sound around me except the rustling of leaves and branches, the occasional bird flying or chirping and the constant noise of the crickets.

None of which help make me feel less tense about my situation. The half-moon is barely illuminating my view. The second I think I spot something larger than a bird, it ends up being another tree after staring at it for a moment and squinting my eyes like a blind person. Which I might be and should be wearing my glasses more often because of, but oh well. I place a hand over my heart while glancing around me for any sort of shape.

Something echoes from behind me and I turn with eyes as wide as saucers. A tall figure stands still a good distance further back from where I came. His tall frame stands before me like a monster ready to hunt me and take me down to hell with him.

A mask on his face, concealing his true self from me. My breath hitches in my throat, not sure what to do. To run or not to run. My mind is screaming that I am in danger and that old flight or fight thing pushes at my thoughts while my entire body freezes in place.

Maybe I am insane. Despite the very evident fear crawling up my spine, there is something else that begs me to run towards the man. I truly have lost my mind. I have been driven to the brink of insanity, I have gone mad. That's it.

Black fabric tight against hard muscles. Concealed identity behind a mask that looks like something straight out of a horror scene. A white mask with black eyes and a stitched up mouth. And one thing I know for certain in this very moment as I stare at the person? Whoever this is, it's not Santino.

Fear blares in the back of my head, my heart beats as fast as it can go, blood pumping through my veins making me feel dizzy. My feet move all on their own, too afraid to know what could happen next. I don't wait for him to make another move towards me as I tale off and start running and running and running until the house becomes a ghost of a memory in the night.

The sound of cracking sticks behind me as he follows right after me, breaths mingled with the soft song of owls and crickets. My hair flying behind me and my eyes stuck in front of me, not even once do I dare to look back until I come to a halt. A small clearance stands before me with grass and a lake or pond in the middle.

Large thick trees covers the forest ground on the other side and more paths leading to who knows where.

"Pretty place, isn't it?" I scream. Five feet from me, maybe less—the guy who chased after me is now before me. The mask now visible. He chuckles. "I see your name even fits. What, backstabbed Santino and decided to have fun by scaring me to death?" I bite. Which seems to make him laugh more, he is enjoying this. What a sick fuck.

"Is that how low you think of me? Although San did warn me about your little mouth, little sex doll, I am not some bastard who shoves knives in his teammates' backs." I glared at him.

"Teammates?" I raise a brow, crossing my arms under my chest. And then, like I've been hit by lighting, the notes from before cross my mind. "Let me calm your mind, little sex doll. No, I didn't stab him in the back. The fucker is pretty much alive and running wild like some hunter looking for a perfect prey to catch." He eyes me up and down and I can practically feel him grinning in this dark mischievous way at me.

"Then what? Why are you here?" I pause. "And stop calling me that." I grit through my teeth.

"Can't enjoy a mere walk through the forest? Aren't you supposed to find Santino, by the way?" He speaks as if it's the brightest fact of the day. Viper stands still, he leans against a thick tree trunk with that fucking mask on his face that not only is creeping me out but has me on high alert the whole time. No matter where I move, he can hear and see me. Despite the night and the lack of light, it seems I am full-on visible to him.

"Why are you out here? Why are you wearing a mask?"

I push my feet to step back as if I am showing bravery instead of pure fear. "As I said, little *sex doll*. I am enjoying a stroll."

"Bullshit." He laughs, head falling back. Sighing, Viper pushes his body away from the tree and walks towards me without stopping. I take a step back, scared of what he might do. Whatever fear-inducing aura Santino has it's less than what this is—this is so much worse. It's dark and corrupting, it's utterly frightening and yet, my body fights every moral thought in my mind.

This fear I have is different than when you know your life is in danger. It's... addictive. I heard the stories, the rumors surrounding the name *Viper*. And no, that isn't his real name. But it is what people know him as.

Viper.

The poison that can kill instantly, the enemy of each human and animal alike. Even the others are scared of him and no one goes against his words. The only one who seems relaxed about his presence is Santino. He seems fine with him, the way he talks about protecting my brother for me had led me to think he has power as well not just Viper.

"You know," he stops just a mere inch from where I stand. With his fist, he pushed my head upwards so I can meet his eyes through the mask. "If I wanted to make you fear me, I could without any issue. Though… if you keep this little scared puppy look up, I might just take that offer. It looks delicious on that pretty face of yours, yum."

"You're fucking insane." I grit my. I am fuelled with more anger and hatred for this asshole.

"And you are utterly mad, Nova." I shudder at how my name rolls off of his lips. His thick rough accent becomes sweet poison to my ears for some reason. "You have every power to stop this and yet you're putting up with it. If you ask me," he comes even closer, our bodies touching while the smell of him wraps around my senses like nothing else in this very second. I feel… dizzy. My mind spirals as I look up from beneath my lashes.

"Fuck," He groans. "Do you know how pretty this face would look covered in cum and tears?" I can *feel* the sadistic grin on his face. My body jerks forward as a soft touch of something creeps up my naked waist. His fingers trace down my lower spine, skin against skin.

"Hmm," His moan echoes in my ears.

"San did say you have a reactive body. I wonder if I grab you and spread you wide right here and now, in front of every animal inside this forest to see, would that pretty tight cunt of yours be wet and dripping? Would it be slick with a need to be fucked raw?" A grip on my neck has my eyes flying wide open.

Shock covers them instead of fear now. That *need* he so elegantly spoke about, it pulls between my legs once more. Why am I reacting to his words like this? I bite my lip, earning a soft chuckle.

"If you could forgive Santino after he fingered your pussy, after he fucked your mouth and filled it with his cum, I am sure you can forgive me, too." He hums in my face, his nose touching my own, our lips so fucking close. I smirk at this words.

"He fucked my pussy, too. Something you can't." He he mocks me with a simple sound. "Hmm," Viper turns me around so fast I get a whiplash. His hard cock pressed against my ass. One hand still wrapped around my throat while his other one dips between my little shorts and cups my aching cunt.

"Not yet. There is time for all of that." He pushes two fingers between my pussy lips, spreading them and driving them as deep as he can go inside of me. His mouth closes around my neck, sucking on the skin and leaving behind a mark. Shit. Santino will hate this. I try to get out, but of course, I fail. My hands wrap around his as I try to pull his hand from my pussy. My body bents forward, pleasure swimming in my belly as I moan from how easily he gets every desired reaction from me. "Stop—hmm, n—ahh!" I feel myself nearing and right as I am on the edge and feel myself coming, Viper stops. He let's go of my neck and steps back, staring at me. His cruel laughter rings through the whole forest. Birds stop chirping and even the sound of crickets vanishes—as if he put them all to sleep. I wanted to curse him out but I fall to my knees instead.

Fuck! I can feel myself soaking my little shorts.

"What a sweet pussy." Viper licks his fingers clean of me. "You should run, little sex doll. You should run and hide as much as you can. I will give you a head count of ten seconds before I start hunting you, too." What?

"Why would you hunt me?" He grins. "Tell me, have you ever been tied up and fucked like a little whore by multiple cocks?" He shakes his head as he answers for me. "No, you haven't."

Viper walks back, one, two, three steps then stops.

"You should run if you don't want to find out how it feels."

And I took off running. I took off running again just like when I spotted him moments ago on the other side of the forest all while his haunting laugh echoes in my head. I run through the thick trees and branched, scratching my thighs in the process. One is deep enough to draw blood. I managed to run a bit more before I started losing sight of everything and had no longer any clue where I was.

Every corner, every branch, every leaf looks the same and I wonder if I am running in circles. I wanted to scream, to yell my safe word yet despite all of that, I *knew* I was safe. I had to be, San wouldn't go that far to make me not feel safe right? Despite hating it, Viper said it as well.

I have power over this game the most. I have power to stop this. And for some reason, I wasn't willing to use it because that would mean this, him and me, it would come to an end and everything would be erased.

Maybe I am mentally sick for wanting this. Maybe my crush on San from back then had developed into something morbid and so twisted that I am willingly allowing myself to get fucked over just to be near him again.

I glance around me, the trees so thick and the night so dark. The fog began pooling around me, cutting my sight even shorter than before. The sound of breaking sticks has my head turning left and right so fast it hurt. I keep thinking that it's either San or Viper. Yet I am met with nothing except a bird flying away or my own feet that I seem to be forgetting about that can make sounds.

I gently tap my hand over my chest where my heart is. "Shh, it's ok, it's ok. It's just nature. I'm just being paranoid, I'm ok."

"Talking to yourself, doll face?" I feel hands wrap themselves around my waist and drag me down to the ground with no mercy. My head hits the soft touch of a hand, shielding me from hitting the hard ground beneath us.

My shirt rises and a pair of burning fingers touches my freezing flesh.

Santino.

He looms above me, dressed in black clothes as well. Not t mention, he had this black ghost face mask on. At first, I wasn't sure if it's him—if it is Santino. However, the spicy woodsy scent mixed with something strong brought this sense of calmness over me and I knew it was him. Not to mention that my body reacts so differently from how it reacts to Viper. The roughness of his touch is there but different. It's a roughness I crave, a merciless kiss I need but am deprived of.

A touch that can burn me and I would be fine with it.

"Whispers are going around that someone else has gotten to you first. Is that so, doll face?" What? Confusion grew on my face before I touched my neck where Viper had left behind a hickey.

"Do not lie to me. Tell me, has someone else put their hands on you?" Did Viper catch Santino? Did he tease him? I feared what that fucker might have told him. I wanted to see his face, I wanted to watch his eyes and not this plastic ghost mask that gave me the utter creeps.

"Don't." My hand stops in mid-air. I cam feel his soft breath fanning over my skin through the holes.

"It stays on unless you use your safe word." My hand falls back to my side softly. "Then everything comes to an end." I nod my head gently, understanding him. Only, I didn't want this game to end.

Chapter 9

Santino pulls me up from the ground, his hand still wrapped around my waist while the other went underneath behind my legs and hoisted me over his shoulder like I weighted nothing.

"Ah!" A scream rang through the dark forest. The world seems to sway before my eyes, the trees end upside down and my hair falls down. I slap Santino's back, my voice muffled by the sudden move.

I manage to push a strand of hair behind my ear, in the far distance, something moves and I spot the odd mask that belonged to Viper. He is watching us, watching me and was laughing most likely. Why is he still here? He isn't going to try something, is he? No, Santino doesn't share, I wasn't going to believe such a thing. I whimper as I felt his rough callused hand land on my bare ass where the shorts stopped covering my skin. The heat of the slap coursed through my body through a shiver.

"W-where are you taking me?" He chuckles.

"To hell, doll face. But the good kind, I promise." My body stiffens for a moment. What does that even mean?

We walked for several minutes, passing through trees and a large graveled pathway leading back to the house. But Santino didn't follow it, he walked right beside it and then swerved right. I spotted the little lake where I stood before. The moonlight shines over it, making it look ethereal in that moment.

Suddenly, something crashes open and Santino wanders inside a small place. It's the wooden hut he told us to stay away from. I'm inside of it. Why am I here? Why had he brought me here? Without missing a beat, Santino drops me on a soft ground and I land with a muffled thud. I hiss in pain from the impact the pillows had over my cut thigh. San grabbed my leg and stretched it out, glancing at the deep cut I got from a branch.

His dark eyes met my light chocolate ones before he pulled my leg up, mask to the side and tongue out. I gasp as he licked the blood up, groaning in pleasure from the metallic taste.

"Do you know how it feels to be sacrificed, doll face?" I felt my eyes go wide in shock. Sacrificed? He wasn't one of those fucked up cult members, was he? Needing a virgin girl to sacrifice to some demon or something? Not that I was a virgin anymore...

"San–"

"You," He bends down on one knee before me, arms caging me in. "You will be tied up and used for pleasure. *Our* pleasure. You will be fucked and filled with cum until that pussy no longer can hold any of it and it starts dripping on the ground in a pool beneath you." His voice is laced with hunger and it burns with desire.

"I will wrap a pretty pink leather strap around your mouth, keeping it wide open for me. While your cunt will be weeping for it to be fucked. To be taken and ruined." He chuckles, a dark sinister sound that sends shivers down my spine.

And despite the fear that seems to be attacking every sane brain cell left, I can only stare and feel excited about it all as I lean slightly back on my hands, watching him. My pussy throbs with each dirty word he speaks. With each soft touch running down my cheek and over to my lips. Santino pulled my bottom lip down with his thumb before shoving it into my mouth. "Suck. Suck like you would my cock."

And I do just that. I bob my head back and forth, wetting the skin with my tongue, using my spit to make it moist and slippery. I taste his skin with my tongue, enjoying every moment. I look up from beneath my semi-wet lashes as tears stings the corners of my eyes for some reason.

"Do not cry. Not yet, at least." He pulls away from me, my mouth open with spit as he uses the pad of his thumb to smudge my saliva over my lips before claiming my mouth hungrily.

"You will look utterly divine once we are done with you."
He talks more to himself, but I still hear him in the quiet little
hut.

We. As in multiple.

The word doesn't register in my head. Santino doesn't hesitate any longer, he grabs my pajama top and rips it open in the
middle with a knife he had hidden in his pocket. The fabric
tears with no issues in one long cut and my shorts follow right
after. My whole body is exposed to him once more. Santino
takes hold of my wrists and wraps a piece of pink ribbon I had
not seen before around them.

He ties it all cutely with a bow as he drags me back up on
my feet and over to a simple little round chair with wooden
feet.

"Stay still, doll face. Just like a sex doll would." To say this
all shocked me was an understatement. I felt a whole different
buzz rushing through my body as this becomes so much more
real.

Fuck!

Ribbons and Rope. It looks like a pretty gift once he is done
with me. *I* look like a pretty gift. Santino grabs my leg and
wraps the rope around it as he bends my ankle towards my ass,
tying knot after knot, braiding the strands and pulling at it tight
enough to secure me but not enough to hurt. His mask covers
his face again, hiding all facial features from me.

"Bend over the chair." He demands. San pulls me up and
forces me to lean over just like he wants me. His hands skilful-

ly wrap the rope around my upper thighs, bringing my ankles all the way up to my ass.

I gasp from the sudden friction over my clit from his knee as it pushes my legs wide open.

"Ah! Fuck." I shudder. "Your wet cunt is begging to be fucked already. Don't worry, you will have every hole taken and stuffed soon." Santino spanks my pussy as I stand spread with him behind me. His fingers tease my clit, rubbing it for a moment and spreading my juices all over my skin. His fingers dive inside me roughly. Pumping in and out.

"What a piece of art. Do you like it, little artist? You're not the only one who can make it." I stare at my thighs, they were covered in rope and Santino started tying little pink bows all around. My cheeks turn a soft red as I lay there with my legs all bent and everything.

"Your hands." I push them forward. He grabbed my wrists, bringing them behind my back. San pulls the same strands from the rope further over my back and around my waist. Using the rest of it to tie knot after knot around my arms and pins them against my back. Going up to my shoulders, he brings the rope forward, gliding it between my breasts, caging them, too.

"Such pretty tits. You know, they would look fucking gorgeous pierced." I shake my head. He laughs. "No? Is that too far?" I wasn't sure. I simply don't like needles. Personally, I have no piercings nor tattoos and when I saw Santino all pierced, my brain reacted differently positively to the sight of it. Curiosity, interest. I wanted to feel his cock pulsating in my mouth, in my dripping pussy. The metal rod hitting every sweet spot possible. I wanted to feel them tickling my inside and I wanted to fucking cum all over them. My thoughts were making me moan and I felt myself trying to shut my legs, trying to stop my wetness from sliding down my ass. I biter my bottom lip.

"Gorgeous." He groans. This was not all, however. I can feel my body being suspended suddenly, the chair vanishes from beneath me. The pull of the rope on my skin tightens a bit which makes the fucker laugh at my reaction. A slight squeal and fear fills me as the idea of being dropped crawls in my mind. "Look at this." That voice followed by that dark stitched-up mask. I catch Viper wandering inside the little hut, walking around me like a predator while Santino steps away and settled on the chair I used to sit on, letting him take a look at his masterpiece.

"You should turn her around. Have her facing the ceiling instead of the ground. Such a perfect view." I stutter as I felt his cold hands touch my waist, doing exactly what he told San to do.

"F-fuck off…" I couldn't speak properly. The hook holding me up was moved around the rope in the middle of my waist and I find myself facing the ceiling—the ceiling that is covered in mirrors. Mirrors that make me stare back at my naked self, at Viper and Santino who both wave at me.

"Don't make me regret letting you keep your voice, muñequita?" Viper's hands touch my burning flesh, I make a move with my ankle, completely forgetting that my legs were tied as I wanted to get away from him. Being naked right now before him was odd yet it turns me on. All of this does, which makes me wonder how fucked up I can be.

"Told you it was a matter of time before I would fuck your pussy, little sex doll." He grins, the humor was audible from behind his mask. Viper then sighs. A fake one. "San told me how you hate me. Had a field day with that news, you know?" His fingers traces one of my breasts, gripping the hard bud and pinching it, slapping it. I cry and moan. "So responsive, too. Fuck this, I love it."

"S–San…"

"Yes, baby?" I whimper as I feel the back of Viper's cold fingers move over my pussy as if he examines me. He plays with my clit, rubbing his thumb over it, making me shake from the teasing feeling.

Pleasure shoots through me but only for a moment as he takes it away from me. Viper pauses as he steps away from me while I am slowly twirled around as he let's go of me. I feel like a disco ball in the club, a puppet in a cage.

"No need to worry, pretty doll. You are safer than safe with me. Ain't that right San?" I felt slightly dizzy as hands cover my nipples, playing with my flesh all bruisingly, picking the hardened bud with his fingers and pinching them until he got every sound out of he wanted.

The sound of mechanics ring around and I am suddenly hoisted in this position where my legs and ass were higher than my head. I feel myself panicking for a second. "Look at this pretty pink pussy all drenched." Viper taunts, his hands touch every inch of me, learning every inch as if he is cramming for an exam. "You know, I'm curious. If you allowed Santino to fuck you while you were still mad at him, I wonder how you will react when I ram my cock in your tight cunt after knowing you despise me to death." He is having a field day with this information so it seems. I want to flip him off so badly.

"You should show her your surprise." San spoke up. Which had Viper nod while humming a yes. "I went and picked it up while he got you all set up for us. Do you like gifts, pretty thing?" Viper asks me. "You need to answer him, use your big girl words for us." I am this close to cursing San out, too.

Yet still, I find myself answering them. "Yes, I do." My voice is weak, soft and barely audible enough.

"Yes what?" Fuck.

"Yes, I do... Masters."

Viper pulls me with him, putting me in a position where I am facing one of the corners of this little place and my lower half faces both of them. Something stands tall before me, covered by a gray piece of cloth. One of them moves around me to pull the fabric off and reveals a large mirror.

The yellowish light barely fills the room, however, it's enough for me to see both men at my feet. Santino tilts his head as he glances at me while Viper is rubbing a hand up and down my thigh, the gift in his hand.

Chapter 10

Chased.

Hunted.

Caught and tied up like a piece of meat to be devoured. Every slow tease of skin over my own, every chuckle that sends shivers over my body. Every soft touch that turns rough and leaves me breathless and wanting more.

I stare at them, at Viper who pulls a box from his pocket and reveals a cute pink toy followed by a small remote.

My gift from him.

"Where does that…" I am no saint, I know what it is. But this one, it feels like it won't go up my pussy but inside—

"Your ass, baby. This will sing a sweet song in your ass. It makes you feel good." Santino nudges his head to Viper and he moves back around me, stopping right by my head. His hand comes down over behind my neck and slightly pulls my head up. Gloved hands now naked, tattoos showing across his half naked body. A leather strap wraps around my face and a metal ring keeps my mouth wide open. My eyes lock on his for a split second before Viper shoves it in my mouth. Once he is done, he moves with the butt plug behind me, coming to a halt between my legs all while Santino watches.

Viper throws the remote over to him and both share a look, I was sure of it.

"Let's test this toy out, huh?" Something cold touches my skin and it wasn't one of them. The sound of something squirting makes me move slightly, curious about what they were doing to my asshole.

"Let's see how it looks. And look, it has a diamond, too." Viper muses.

His fingers move over what I think must be lube. Massaging my hole with one finger. Viper holds my waist with one hand while stretching me out first. I shake, my head falling back as my eyes go wide. I try to move from his touch, try to make it less feel less full of his finger and toy but my moan gives away just how much I love it.

"Breathe, you are fine," I mumble a cry as I try to grab hold of my mind only to have him add a second finger and this time, they moved deeper. I feel full almost immediately.

They laugh at my reaction. They enjoy it so much, watching me, teasing me. Fuck! I can't stand it anymore. I feel my lower region throbbing with need. I need to feel something, anything that can get rid of that ache. My eyes glance back at myself in the mirror bestie me and at the ones above me. The large body mirror shows both of them as they stare at me. Viper pulls his fingers out and a second later, the push of the toy has me crying. My eyes close on their own from both pleasure and from the slight discomfort. And of course, I get scolded by Santino because of it.

"Keep your eyes open, muñequita. Or he stops." The movement slows down for a second until I open my eyes again.

"Pesh." I try to beg.

That failed. Whatever word came out, I sounded like an incoherent person. I watch myself in the state I am in. Spread open wide, tied up, wet and aching, teased and marked from earlier games.

"What a sick little girl. Begging to be fucked by two men. What a whore." I drop my head back, my hair falling like curtains behind me. Santino walks up to me, placing a hand over my throat, squeezing it tightly and cutting my air supply off just enough to put pressure and make my heart hammer behind my ribcage.

"Do you see yourself, doll face?" He whispers in my ear as he bends down beside me. I feel both of them right now, their touches driving me insane, pushing me over the edge of insanity as they were barely giving me anything to put me out of this misery. I watched myself just as he told me to.

"Do you see how fucking erotic you look?" I nod as his eyes land on mine through the mirror.

Viper grins, his chest moving as he laughs. "Let me show you how good you look when fucked by us." There is no waiting, no patience or any sign of them slowing down once they began. In the next second, Santino grabs my head, releasing the pink belt around my head and brings his cock right to my lips, pushing himself in my open mouth. The thick bulge is too much, the pressure making me fold and shake, my voice reverberating through the dark hut, the sound tickling him while my eyes close on their own again.

"So soft..." San groans. Viper on the other hand, he grips my waist tightly. My shoulders tense up, my legs aching from how they were tied up. Saliva drips down the side of my mouth as his cock reaches the back of my throat just like he likes it. Viper's fingers find my clit, rubbing it in circles and making me twitch from that tight feeling that takes over. Once he sees I am ready, he replaces his fingers with his cock.

Viper teases my hole first, pushing just the tip in at first before going further. My moans, pleas and cries echo in the room, eyes rolling back from the feeling of both of their cocks claiming me.

"Ah!" I scream as the toy starts vibrating in my ass. The feeling of it tickles my walls and I'm not sure what to do as the sensation intensifies to the point I forget how to breath or how to think. I can't escape this no matter what I do or try to do at least. Each shake of my body, each try to flee has them laughing with pleasure. I am still adjusting to Viper's size ramming into me. Santino has a long thick shaft with veins and piercings as far as I remember. And Viper isn't far either, thick and maybe a bit shorter in length than San, though this doesn't mean he isn't big and that it doesn't fill me up just as fast as Sandino's cock did when he fucked me in his office.

I gag on San as he pushes himself even deeper to the point I start seeing black starts. He doesn't slow down until I feel him coming and filling my mouth. A mixture of both cum and saliva drips down my face, some lands on the ground. I try to swallow but I end up chocking because of the way I'm hanging.

"So soft, so easy to bend and use. I bet you like being used like this, huh?" Viper spanks my ass when I don't answer and the toy start going crazy. "Being fucked roughly by two animals. Being taken and controlled." Viper keeps commenting. His voice rough and filled with pleasure as he taunts me. Degrades me in anyway he wishes and all I do is sit pretty and take it all like a good girl.

"Fuck! Doll face, this mouth is heaven." San groans louder and louder with each thrust driving deeper and deeper. He goes again, taking my mouth until he fills me throat once more.

"Look at the sight of you. Look at the type of slut you are. Taking the cocks of people you barely know, people you hate. Look at how you look all tied up. What a good little slut." The words drive me mad. Santino agrees, adding his own degrading words mixed with praise.

They were right though. I am a dirty little slut. And that makes me clench my walls around Viper's cock as he keeps fucking me and makes me cum so hard I start to cry. Literal tears drip from my eyes and I want nothing more than to fall and be held tightly. His own cum fills me to the brim as he ruts deep and without breaking the pace. If it weren't for me being tied up and held up in the air, I might have fallen to the ground a long time ago. My body aches from how I am tied and the lack of space to move turned my muscles numb.

Yet these demons could care less. Right now, right here. All they care about is claiming me and fucking me wild until I became an utter mess covered in *their* cum.

Once they are done fucking their chosen holes, they switch places.

I try speaking, only to have my words muffled by Viper's cock. His body is covered in tattoos from head to toe. His chest his arms, every inch of his skin is covered. Painting after painting, words with meaning and—Fuck! My eyes glide down all the way to his cock he pushes in and out of my mouth. A small star shape I don't have enough time to check out. My thoughts are stopped as he shoves my mouth open by grabbing my hair from the lower back, making me hiss in pain.

"So wet and hot. Fuck damn." My tongue darts out, the mixture of saliva and San's cum now becoming lube for Viper's cock. I wrap my lips around his shaft, veins touching my tongue. I feel myself slipping. I a, already overstimulated from the toy, the fingering, the fuck session. My pussy is sore from being taken so roughly the whole day. And yet I don't do anything to stop it. I single my fingers, my own moans gets mixed up with their groans and cries of pleasure as they cum and fill me up again and again.

Santino picks up where Viper left off. Pushing himself in me as deep as he can go. His balls hit the toy in my ass that is going in these breaking buzz-like sounds. Almost as if it's choking—and it doesn't help the tension and the pleasure I am feeling. My eyes land on the mirror once more, I am a full mess of cum, spit, and tears just how they promised I would end up.

I shake my head when Viper takes his cock out, giving me a second to breathe.

"Good girl, you're doing such a good job." In the mirrors above us, Santino is no longer dressed in his his pants, they are discarded somewhere and so were Viper's. Tattoos in full view. I watched my upside-down self. Yes. My face is tattooed across his chest above his heart. For some reason the sight of it does something to my heart, it makes it beat fast and it aches at the same time. Before I can wrap my brain round it, San slams into me once, twice, three times in rough beats. Every thought turns to a hushed nothing. Every dirty word turns me into easily mouldable play-doh.

"This fucking pussy is heaven. So tight. Hmm, yes! Fuck, yes!" I shudder. Santino's cock pulsates inside me. The knot breaks and both of us come at the same time. Viper isn't far behind us, his pre-cum slides down and several strokes later he explodes in my mouth. His seed drips down the side of my mouth, over my cheeks and on the ground.

"Be a good little slut and swallow, little sex doll." The rope from above drops and I fall to the ground on something soft. The pillows were still there and they catch my fall again. Viper moves over to turn me on my stomach. The ropes from around my hands go loose and I whimper as the flesh feels tender and my muscles ache from being forced into one position. I feel the soft touch of lips abasing my burning flesh.

Viper kissed my wrists.

San moves my body up, having me lean against his chest as he unwraps the rest of the ropes and ribbons from my legs next and helped me stretch them. I watched carefully as Viper changes positions and sits before me, spreading my legs softly and glanced at the cum spilling out of my pussy.

"Such a wasteful little girl. You should be more careful, here let me help you." With two fingers, he wet them in his mouth and pushes the cum back inside of me. Santino grabs my wrists, pushing his legs between my own as he settles me on his lap and spread them wide for Viper to do his thing. His fingers curled inside of me once again, thumb touching my clit as he rubs my sweet spot. My mouth falls open in an O shape.

I am so damn sensitive, my insides are tender from being fucked by both of them and this little friction has me instantly coming.

"Wait—no, yes—" I stutter. I' not sure what I want to say but I said something that had them snickering, grinning like foxes. I have no idea when they took their masks off but I could care less, finally I can see them again.

"Is it a no? Or a yes? Do you want him to stop, baby?" I bite my bottom lip. Whining as I try to focus but couldn't. Viper slowly twists his fingers inside me, feeling the walls around his fingers tightening as I feel myself coming a second time form just this.

"I think she wants you to stop, V." I desperately shale my head no. "No! No, no, no. Please, please, please make me come again, please." My breaths are ragged, my stomach moving back and forth as I try to control my breathing. Viper sucks his teeth, making that tsk sound. "You want me to make you come? I thought you hated me?" I shake my head, if he keeps going at this soft pace, I am going to start kicking his ass. I need more of it, more of this pleasure and fast. I feel my pussy throbbing, sucking on his fingers as if it were his cock.

"You don't?" He teases. Eyes staring down at me with lust.

"NO! I don't." I moan. "I'm sorry, master. Please forgive me, please make me come."

"You want to come?" I nodded again. "Yes, please. Make me your cum dumpster. I'll be a good girl. Please."

"Come on, V. Look at the mess you created. You should reward her. Eat her pussy." I move away from the feeling of the toy buzzing back to life again only to have San grab my wrists and pin me down against his chest, his cock against my ass.

Viper settled down on his knees, wrapping his arms around my upper thighs and pulling my legs open as his tongue darts out and licks over my clit Ince single swipe, sending shivers and shudders through me.

Chapter 11

Santino nuzzles his head in the crook of my neck. His mouth licks at my skin, biting the flesh and branding it with his teeth.

Viper on the other hand is biting on my clit, pulling at the skin before slurping my juices and cum up. I feel his fingers dive deeper, from two fingers there were three and I can't help move lower body, pulling away only to be pinned down by both of them.

"Stay still, pretty girl and let me eat." I suck in a breath, biting my bottom lip hard I can feel the soft cushion breaking, tasting metal. San grabs my face in his hand and pulls my lip free only to smash his mouth on me. His tongue breaks past my lips and in my mouth. I moan into our kiss, eyes rolling back. The feeling of him exploring me, the feeling of Viper touching me with his tongue after pulling his fingers from my cunt. It's a pleasure that drives me utterly mad and I can't hold myself up anymore. I am leaning against Santino, no longer strong enough to be able to do something and that is all they need to continue playing with me until I'm utterly at their mercy.

"Come…" I mutter against San's lip. "Are you going to come, doll face?" I nod. My voice is hoarse from screaming and moaning.

"Did you hear that Viper? You are making her come."

"Be a good girl then and come all over my face. Cover me in your sweet desire, cover this bastard's face all up." The hate sex is one thing they were right about when they wrote about it in books. A hate fuck session is fucking *brilliant*.

I feel my body shake, the knots breaking and I beg them to let me go while they keep touching me more and more.

The second we are done, I finally take a moment to breath and gather my thoughts. The mirrors are covered in fog, the toy is hidden from me and I'm placed on the couch in the corner. My mouth, my pussy, my ass. All filled with their seeds. I don't know how many hours it had been since they caught me, I am sure it's near the middle of the night, right?

It had to be. They were able to take turns so many times and they weren't even tired. Barely breaking a sweat. I lean over the couch's armrest, pressing my head down into my arm and rested there with my legs curled up near me while Viper took care of me and cleaned me up. Santino helps me drink some water and hands me his hoodie while a blanket covers my legs once V is done. Soft touches and little sweet kisses cover my back. One hand or finger—I wasn't sure, rubs over my spine as the feeling of the cold night air slips inside through the now open door and has me shivering.

"Is she on the pill?" Viper asks from behind the couch as he comes back. He is dressed in his jeans again, no shirt.

"No." San answers with no hesitation.

"Good." V states, earning a grin from San. "May the best man win, then." Viper chuckles, massaging a hand through my hair. "I have a mission for you and I down in Vegas. I will call you on Monday after they leave."

Santino woken me up a moment later, my mind still replaying the scenes from moments ago. My ankles hurt and I hiss when I stand back up. My pussy aches, my skin stings. Watching me from the corner of the room where he placed the items used on me on the wooden chair, Santino walks over and picks me up bridal style.

"Ah! W—where are we going?" He kisses my lips first before speaking.

"To sleep." He walks out of the little hut and back to the house. The lights are back on, Viper had gone to the kitchen and we went upstairs. I glanced over San's shoulder and over to where the other one was. His eyes watched me, a mischievous look in his eyes. I hide my face from him by using Santino's neck.

"What time is it?"

"It's four in the morning." I stared in awe at him. He laughs, his head falling back as I am placed down on the large bed.

"Aren't you…" I began. He turns back around, his half-naked body faces me and I can't help but let my eyes roll down over every inch of him. Over his tattoos, over my face I see just slightly, old Greek numerals on his right abdomen in small that I am sure is some sort of date, there are some roses on his left arm, his fingers covered in more numbers.

Tattoos over tattoos. Skulls among the roses, two birds on his abdomen pointing down to his V-Line.

"You should rest up first, I might not be able to hold myself from touching you otherwise. Besides, I need to send the fucker off."

I want to roll my eyes, instead, I settle for a small nibble of my bottle lip as I lay down on the bed, dragging the covers over my body with a slight hiss.

"Do not blame me for your lack of being able to hold your urges. You also must be insane for being able to still go after *hours* of going at it." He chuckles as he walks over to me and settles on the edge of the bed. "You are my insanity, doll face. My deprived and sick obsession next to everything else." Now I roll my eyes. Which earned me a warning look. He watches me. "Fuck, doll face. I shouldn't want you this much."

I smile wickedly. Though… I know better then to let that prideful feeling take over. I sigh. "We need to talk," He agrees. "That we do. But later. Right now, I need you to relax." I nod again. Santino taps my nose and leaves the room. The door remains open wide though. I spot something in the corner of the room. A camera, slightly shifting and for a second I feel embarrassed. I know he has cameras everywhere. There is one in my room, too. Chase, however, told me it was shut off for my privacy and would be turned on when we left.

Lies.

I understand why someone like him would have security everywhere. I lean back against the pillow. My mind drifts to old thoughts for a second as I stay under the warm cover until I decide to grab a shower inside San's room.

I dry my body with a towel and walk back into the bedroom. I know I am supposed to rest but I needed that shower badly. I flicked the switch I found near the door on and looked around the room, taking every corner in. Except for the things already inside his room, there is nothing else. Another door on the wall next to the bathroom leads me to the walk-in closet with two sides. One room is empty and larger, with a built-in vanity and I can't help but stare in awe at how pretty it is.

There are a few things around like a vase with flowers, a pair of diamond earrings, a necklace and a red box with a black ribbon tied in a pretty bow ion top of the island in the middle of the closet. I am curious to see what is inside, however, chose against it since it isn't mine. I only know it's from a famous fashion house that sells clothes for women. A brand that feels familiar to me for some reason.

I wonder if it belongs to some fling or ex-lover or something. Despite Santino not looking like the type of person who would feel something beyond a lustful emotion, he is a closed-off book that makes it hard for me to figure out what he is truly thinking. So the thought doesn't leave me about him having someone. Or having *had* someone. I gripped the towel tighter around my chest, my naked feet tapping over the wooden floorboard as I look through his side of the closet for a shirt since I put the other one in the basket with dirty clothes.

The glass case closet on my right, at the end of the room with the weapons is still left open. I walk closer and touch the cold case. This house is beautiful, everything about it is beyond my imagination. This little corner kind of goes against the beauty of this place

"Beautiful aren't they?" Startled, I glance behind me only to spot Santino leaning against the door frame.

"Why do you have them out in the open? Isn't it dangerous? Someone could try and break in, use them." He let's a soft sound out that mimics a laugh. He walks closer, caging me in his arms as they wrap around my waist and leans his head into the crook of my neck. The smell of him, his minty breath and the mix of his cologne turn my mind mushy again.

Dangerous game. This man is driving me insane and it's just the first day that I am seeing him again. *Feeling* him after last time.

"Thinking about pulling the trigger on me, doll face?" I roll my eyes and laugh it off as I turn around and push myself from his body where it is warm. "No. I barely can hold a knife and use it properly when cooking. Never mind fire a gun." He eyes me. Those deep dark eyes narrow on my movements as he stares at my fingers were old cuts from when Chase had me help him on a mission has left behind marks. The cuts came from little incisions the doctors did on fixing broken finger bones. I wore little casts followed by a bigger one around my arm for six months. It took me a year to finally regain full control of the paintbrushes and even so, my paintings were odd. Odd with unsteady strokes. They made the end result look unfit or weak. To my utter surprise, the teacher had called them beautiful.

Hands are an artist's most prized possessions. Whether working with clay or painting, writing… anything. Santino kisses my fingers but doesn't say anything.

"Why's the other closet empty?" I try to change the subject to something else. Maybe this way I can get some answers and learn who Santino truly is.

"Because there is no woman who has claimed that room yet. I'm hoping to change that after tonight." I can feel the grin on his lips as I watch the door to the other closet. The box and the jewelry made me wonder until my thoughts are cut off by Santino dragging the towel from my body and placing a shirt of his over my naked self.

"I could fuck you with this shirt on." He growls in my ear, making my cheeks flush red.

"You would like that, wouldn't you?" He nods, staring at me with hunger in his eyes and cock getting hard again, rubbing against my pussy. I bite my lip, lean my head back. My mouth parts and a soft moan escapes me.

Epilogue

"And then Chase and Jax had decided it would be smart to mix several drinks before they passed out like idiots." I glance at Cole as he walks downstairs around twelve o'clock. The guys had come home around five or so in the morning and Santino had dragged their asses upstairs with Cole's help who was done with the partying and wanted to sleep.

I went back to Santino's bedroom once he was done. The room is so dark with the pulled curtains that I end up walking into the side of the bed like a fool. San snickers from behind me as he walked over to me and checks my toes out after turning the bedside lamp on.

"I don't know your room. I didn't realize the bed was that far in the room." He shakes his head.

"You should hang out more here to learn the layout of the room then." Is he...?

"Are you inviting me back?"

"Maybe I am. What will you do?" I thin my lips, trying to hide my smile from him. "Only if I get to come back alone, maybe I will think about it."

San laughs, shaking his head. "And here I thought you love your brother." I laugh as I settled back in bed. I turn around, teasing him a bit by bending my chest forward and flexing my ass slightly in his face. His hand comes down on my behind and I giggle at the rough yet gentle spanking.

"What a fucking tease."

Later that day, I joined Santino in the kitchen around twelve to make lunch for everyone. I had fallen asleep in his arms early this morning after everything. And when I woke up, San was beside me typing some emails on his phone with my head on his lap while he stroked one hand through my hair.

"Cannot believe you guys got me into drinking those shitty drinks." Cole sits down on the chair beside me around the island as I pierce the fruit on my plate and dip it into the white chocolate lathered over my pancakes. I stare at Santino on the other side of the island, licking the sauce just like how I had done with his cum. His eyes watch me and I can see his Adam's apple bobbing as he swallows the dryness from his mouth away.

I almost laugh. Teasing him is so damn fun since he can't do anything to me right now. He decided to enjoy some extra minutes with me after I woke up again while everyone was still sleeping by fingering me before slipping his cock inside and fucking me. I barely was able to hold my moans in as he trusted in me with so much force, so much hunger for me that it shook the bed and made it hit the wall.

"Should I ask?" Cole takes a sip from his coffee as he settled down next to me again. I shake my head. "Did you guys enjoy last night?"

For some reason, I think is see Cole tensing up. I raise my brows, staring at his face that barely had any emotion on it. Santino shakes his head at him, stepping from the island to lean against the other side of the counter where the cooking plate is now cooling off after he is done making pancakes for us.

"I'm being switched over to New Richdale's base in three weeks." Cole suddenly speaks up, cutting the silence off. "But didn't you get transferred to London like a year or so ago?" Cole shrugs his shoulders.

"Viper's orders." I stop speaking as Chase walks down into the kitchen dressed in only a pair of shorts. Several hickeys cover his neck and his chest. Bite marks—teeth marks coating his flesh. Slightly bigger marks than a normal girl's mouth…

I glance at my brother as an odd expression crosses his soft features.

Something is bothering him and he stares at Cole who doesn't give him any attention while he sips his coffee. Sadly, until my brother is close to exploding from too many feelings, I can't get a word out of him. I sigh, pause my train of thoughts and decide to focus on my food while the others started coming down as well, chatter finally filling the kitchen.

"Does everyone have everything they need? Tickets, rides?" We all nod. Chase had rented a car for us, so we had to leave an hour early for the airport tonight. I walk back to my room later once we are done to finish packing. And Santino dropped in like some sick puppy.

"I wish you could stay." He mutters, wandering inside the room and wrapping his arms around my waist from behind. Nuzzling his head in the crook of my neck, kissing my skin before giving me another kiss on the lips.

"I'm gonna miss the sun..." I pout, warning me a squeeze around my waist and a bite on my neck.

"Ouch. That hurts."

"Then you shouldn't be that bratty." I playfully glare at him as I turn around in his arms. I jump on my tippy–toes, pecking his lips quickly, making him chuckle while he shakes his head at me.

"Is that a kiss?" I hum a yes. "Let me show you what a kiss is, baby." Lips crash against each other, teeth abasing teeth, hands diving underneath my shirt over my breasts and gripping them. Fingers tracing the hard buds before dipping under my skirt and rubbing my clit.

"So wet, so fucking responsive. Should I tell Viper how wet you are when he calls later?"

An idea popped into my head instead. I grab his phone from his pocket and turn around to face the mirror of the closet. I open the camera, staring at my shirt ridden over my chest, my breast out of my green lace bra.

"Such pretty tits." His hand wraps around my large cups. I am blessed in this department. His other hand is in my panties, fingers inside of me. I click the record button and film San fingering me. I try my best to cover my moans by slapping my hand over my mouth. The video is cut short since I lose control over my hands and need to hold onto something.

"Here, this would be even better." San drops me on the ground, ass up and panties to the side as they are covered in my juices, drenched in it actually. San records more of this dirty play and my moans can be heard in the background of the video.

"And look at that. He already hearted it. The fucker." I flip him off as I come down from my high. "Careful, baby. Or I might shive that finger someone." I pout.

"What a cute pout you have. Shall I fuck it?" He grins like a wolf. Of course, he wants to fuck my mouth as well. His sex drive was over the moon. San's fingers are coated in my juices and I suck them clean. San's fingers are coated in my juices and I suck them clean before he can stop me. I bob my head up and down, moaning in pleasure and so does he.

San helps me up and I lean into his embrace for as long as I can until Chase breaks in and I almost jump out of my skin. He eyes me for a second but something else plays in his mind, not caring enough about what might have happened between Santo and I.

"We need to, um…" San eyes him. "We'll talk later," San whispers to me and I nod.

This is fucking Insane.

I'm utterly insane.

And Santino, Viper, they are driving me deeper into this insanity with them.

About the author

Writing red flags with gentleman acts and the occasional burning down the world for their girl is what this author does best!

...

Maddie C. is a dark indie romance author who loves diving into the twisted beauty of love, pain, and desire. Her stories blend raw emotion with atmospheric depth, pulling readers into shadowy worlds where nothing is ever simple, especially the heart.

When she's not writing, Maddie fuels her creativity through baking, spending time with her family and friends and cuddling with her loyal fur baby. She believes the best stories come from a mix of imagination, experience, and a little chaos.

Do you want to be the first to know about Maddie. C's next release or stay up to date for more fun stuff?

Follow Author Maddie. C on her social media!

Instagram: authormaddie.c
TikTok: authormaddie.c